Praise for Pam

"Fast paced and ~~entertaining~~"
—*Romantic Times BOOKreviews* on
The Wedding Heiress

"Delightfully amusing...a 'not to be missed'
book by first-rate author Pamela Ford."
—*CataRomance Reviews* on
The Wedding Heiress

"Upbeat, witty and as much fun as the
merry-go-round...I loved it."
—*Romance Reader at Heart* on
The Wedding Heiress

"Ms. Ford has delivered a truly delightful take.
The Sister Switch is definitely headed
for this reviewer's keeper shelf."
—*Romance Readers Connection*

"The dialogue between her characters
sparkles."
—*Romantic Times BOOKreviews* on
The Sister Switch

"A warm-hearted family story, a sweet
feel-good romance...a thoroughly
enjoyable book."
—*Romance Reviews Today* on
The Sister Switch

Dear Reader,

As I wrap up the finishing touches on this, my fifth novel for Harlequin Superromance, I am reminded of how fortunate I am to be writing for Harlequin Books. Though I didn't discover romance fiction until my late twenties, once I did, I was hooked. I still remember reading my first romance novel—a historical—and wondering how I, an insatiable reader, had managed to miss this genre for so long. These were uplifting stories about women rising above adversity, taking charge of their lives, having adventures, raising children and falling in love. Who could ask for more?

Making up for lost time, I began reading romances by the armful and soon decided I wanted to write them as well. My first couple of efforts were truly learning experiences, but by the third book, I managed to pull all the pieces into a novel that Harlequin wanted to buy. The day I got that call was one I will never forget. I am thrilled to be part of the Harlequin sisterhood (men included!) of readers, writers and publishing professionals, and I know, without a doubt, that the insight and input of my editors has helped make my books better.

I hope you enjoy *Her Best Bet,* a story about dreams, how they can change and how we discover what we truly want only once we look into our hearts. I love hearing from readers; please e-mail me at pamelaford@pamelaford.net or through my Web site at www.pamelaford.net.

All the best,

Pamela Ford

Her Best Bet
Pamela Ford

HARLEQUIN®

TORONTO • NEW YORK • LONDON
AMSTERDAM • PARIS • SYDNEY • HAMBURG
STOCKHOLM • ATHENS • TOKYO • MILAN • MADRID
PRAGUE • WARSAW • BUDAPEST • AUCKLAND

Recycling programs
for this product may
not exist in your area.

ISBN-13: 978-0-373-71593-0

HER BEST BET

www.eHarlequin.com

Printed in U.S.A.

ABOUT THE AUTHOR

Award-winning author Pamela Ford spent many years writing for advertising agencies and corporations before chasing down her dream of becoming a freelance writer and novelist. Ever the romantic, she is already hard at work on her next novel. She loves to hear from readers and can be e-mailed at pamelaford@pamelaford.net or reached through her Web site www.pamelaford.net.

Books by Pamela Ford

**HARLEQUIN
SUPERROMANCE**

Don't miss any of our special offers. Write to us at the following address for information on our newest releases.

Harlequin Reader Service
U.S.: 3010 Walden Ave., P.O. Box 1325, Buffalo, NY 14269
Canadian: P.O. Box 609, Fort Erie, Ont. L2A 5X3

To Teri Wagner and Susan Mongoven,
who are truly angels on Earth.

And to Bob, because you're the best.

Acknowledgments

My thanks to the following people for sharing their
knowledge so this story could become a reality:

Don Ford, Mel Pike,
Mike Chmurski at Megel Corporation
and Barry Mainwood at Mainly Editing.

CHAPTER ONE

ON A BRIGHT SATURDAY MORNING in August, Elizabeth Gordon opened her mail, spilled her coffee and came face-to-face with her life. It wasn't pretty.

The dark liquid raced across the letter she laid open on the kitchen table and poured over the edge like a mini-waterfall to the scuffed hardwood floor below. She jumped to her feet and snatched a handful of napkins from the holder, blotting at the spill as though she could lift the words from that single sheet and make them disappear. As if it would make her forget what she had just read…

Dear Izzy,
If you've gotten this letter, it means you're coming up to your ten-year high school reunion. Can you believe it, Iz? You've been out of high school ten years already. So, here's what you're doing for a living right now: you're a movie director. Or, okay, maybe an assistant director. That'd be all right, too. Or even an assistant-to-an-assistant. As long as you're doing what you want to do—and not what Mom and Dad want. Tell me you didn't marry some guy *they* thought was perfect and become a trophy wife. On a shelf. With 2.5 perfect

kids. Because, Izzy, if you did, I don't know what I'll do. I'm eighteen. I'm about to graduate from high school and go to college. I don't want a husband. I want to do something fun, exciting, rewarding. I want to work in film. *You* want to work in film. So, Izzy, that's your future. The movies! I can't wait to get there. I can't wait to read this in ten years and know that I'm doing something I love—just like they said I couldn't.

Love and kisses, xxxooo from yourself,
Izzy

It had been an English class assignment her senior year—write a letter to yourself describing what your life would be like in ten years. The teacher had collected the letters and said they would be mailed out with the reunion invitation.

She'd forgotten all about it. Slowly she lowered herself back into her chair. *What had happened to her dreams?* Somehow she'd fallen into a lifestyle—pattern—*rut*. How had she let her life come to this, this moment where her loss of direction seemed exquisitely obvious? Suddenly she had the sensation that she was floating, looking down at herself like they say you do when you die.

"Izzy?"

She felt herself snap back into her body and focused on the willowy blonde in the doorway, her roommate, Shelly Kent. Though Shelly had the fine-boned features of a model, she rarely wore makeup outside of work and paid just enough attention to fashion to make sure she wasn't out of style.

"The mail came already?" Wrapped in a pink cotton robe, Shelly padded toward her and reached for the short pile of bills and junk mail.

"Yeah." Years were passing her by and she hadn't even noticed. *Dreams were passing her by.* She'd meant to get into film and instead… She cringed.

"What's wrong with you?" Shelly glanced up from the mail. "Did you get on the scale this morning? Because I thought we decided we'd only weigh in every—"

"I'm the traffic manager at a little cable TV station," Izzy said with disdain. *"Traffic manager."*

"So?"

"So? I manage the video inventory. I maintain the advertising logs. I schedule on-air promotion. I don't do anything remotely related to making movies."

"And I'm the weather girl. A weather girl—not a movie star."

"Yeah, but traffic manager was never on my list of dreams. Weather girl was on yours."

"Only if I didn't make it as a movie star. And you may have noticed, Hollywood hasn't come calling yet, but when they do, I'll be ready. Until then, it's cumulus clouds for me." Shelly poured herself a cup of coffee, refilled Izzy's mug and slid into the seat opposite. "I'm sure traffic manager is on somebody's list of dreams—just add it to yours. So, what's this really about?"

Izzy picked up the damp paper and slapped it on the table in front of Shelly. "Read this. How would you feel if you got this in the mail?"

As Shelly read the letter, she pressed her lips together. "Like a loser. Especially if I got to my reunion and discovered everyone else had succeeded beyond their wildest dreams."

"Thanks."

Shelly pushed her chin-length hair behind one ear and took a sip of her coffee. "I was kidding. I'm sure it won't be like that. When you're eighteen you don't know anything about life. You didn't have a clue how hard it would be to break into directing—"

"I hardly tried. My parents knew the manager at the cable station, so I landed there—and stayed. Dreams be damned, it was just easier. You were right the first time. *Loser.* At least I have a boyfriend."

Shelly made a gagging sound. She tilted her head thoughtfully for a long moment. Then she shoved back her chair, pushed up her robe sleeves and began to pick through the garbage in the wastebasket beneath the sink.

"There's food in the pantry. Just because we're dieting doesn't mean you have to resort to scraps."

"Ha-ha. I finally sorted that mountain of old junk mail and magazines on my nightstand yesterday," Shelly said, still digging. "And wouldn't you know it, today I need something I threw away. You always wonder why I keep all that stuff for so long, well, this is why. Because— Here it is!" She pulled a brochure from the bag and wiped a swath of coffee grounds off the front.

"Here what is?"

"Your salvation. The Americana Documentary Film Contest for amateur and student filmmakers."

Coffee cup halfway to her mouth, Izzy froze. "What?"

"Now, if we have any luck at all…" Shelly opened the brochure and scanned the copy. "Thank goodness. The Outline Submission Round doesn't close for four days."

Izzy almost choked on her coffee. "Are you out of your mind?"

"Do you want to go to your class reunion as the person who didn't even try to follow her dreams? They'll probably be displaying everyone's letters and goals in some big PowerPoint presentation." Shelly waved a hand through the air. "I can almost see it. Column one—what each person wanted to do. Column two—a gold star for success and a sad face for you, because the one thing you accomplished was the only thing you told yourself *not* to do—settle down with some guy your parents thought was perfect."

Izzy stared, dumbfounded, as her friend kept talking without waiting for an answer.

"Let's try this, Izzy. All we need to do is submit a one-to-two-page summary describing the documentary film we want to make if we get chosen to progress to the Video Submission Round."

"We?"

Shelly grinned. "*We,* baby. You want to be a director. I want to be a star. We might as well chase our dreams together."

Izzy snorted. "Go back to bed and get some more sleep. You're delirious."

"Delirious? Replace the *r* with a *c* and I'm *delicious.*"

"Ohmigod."

"Face it, Iz, it's an absolutely delicious idea. And

since we're practically starving ourselves to lose ten pounds, *delicious* is a word I'd like to have in my vocabulary right now even if it only relates to making a movie."

This was absurd. Totally and absolutely absurd. And totally and absolutely tempting. "What happens if we progress to the Video Submission Round?"

"I thought you'd never ask." Shelly turned her attention back to the brochure. "Two weeks after the Outline Submission Round closes, ten entrants will be selected as finalists by a panel of judges," she read aloud. "Finalists will have two months to create a six-minute short documentary expressing the topic presented in their outline."

The idea began to cozy its way deeper into her mind. "And the winners are announced…when?"

Shelly dropped into her chair and tossed the brochure on the table. "Ten days after that. This whole contest will be wrapped up in three months—in plenty of time for your class reunion. Feels like it was meant to be, doesn't it?"

"I'm merely asking a couple of questions. I'm not actually considering it. I mean, what would Andrew think?"

"Andrew would think you're being silly and impulsive, that you don't have a prayer of winning so why enter, that if you become a finalist, you won't have as much free time to be the perfect girlfriend to him." Shelley slowly straightened in her chair and raised her coffee cup. "Who cares what Andrew thinks?"

"Well, I—"

"No! No, you don't! Come on, Izzy, it's the chance of

a lifetime. You get to follow your dreams and I get to be on film discussing something other than weather patterns."

Izzy pursed her lips and silently debated whether her roommate was brilliant or deranged. There was such a fine line between the two.

"And, it could be a real boon for your career. I mean, think if we won. Doors would open—"

"*Could* open." Izzy stood and refilled her mug. Shelly could be on to something. Or not. She did have a penchant for jumping to wild conclusions.

"*Likely* open. For both of us. No more traffic managering for you. No more weather girl for me." She arched a hand through the air. "From now on it'll be top billing for both of us! Come on, Izzy, help me out here."

"Shelly, what if—"

"What could possibly go wrong?"

Actually, she couldn't think of a thing, short of Andrew getting exasperated with her. But if they finaled, Andrew's exasperation would be the least of her concerns. The corners of her lips curved upward as she considered what it would feel like to attend her reunion with her head held high, as a finalist—maybe even the winner—of a documentary film contest.

"What have we got to lose?"

Nothing. She exhaled. "Okay, we'll write an outline."

"We will?" Shelly jumped to her feet and danced over to give Izzy a hug. "You're the best!"

"Oh, stop. Just two pages, right? On any American topic?"

"That's what it says. Got any thoughts?"

"I don't know… Football? That's pretty American."

Shelly stuck two pieces of wheat bread in the toaster. "Football skews male. What if some of the judges are female? How about apple pie?"

"Skews female. And boring."

For the next several minutes they bandied about ideas, discarding each in turn for one reason or another.

"What about that property your parents own? That old resort up in Wisconsin." Shelly sprinkled cinnamon and sugar on the toast and handed a piece to Izzy. "Isn't that place steeped in Americana?"

Izzy shrugged. "They don't own the resort—only the land. And they're selling that, anyway. My great-great-grandfather gave some guy a hundred-year lease and finally it's coming due."

"Hmm. That could be an interesting angle."

"Yeah, well, the broker told my parents it's getting run-down. Who wants to see a documentary about a seedy resort?"

"No one," Shelly said glumly.

Izzy bit into her toast. A memory of her grandfather telling stories of the old days popped into her mind. Unless… "Unless the documentary isn't about the resort. What if it's about the gangsters?"

"What gangsters?"

"My grampa used to tell me stories that his father told him. About growing up there during the twenties. How the gangsters from Chicago used to come to northern Wisconsin for vacations and—"

"You mean like Al Capone?"

"Yeah. And John Dillinger and Baby Face Nelson and—"

"Are you kidding me?" Shelly set her coffee cup on

the table and leaned forward onto her elbows. "Did they ever stay at your resort?"

"It's not our resort—"

"Yeah, yeah, only the land. Did they ever stay there?"

"That's what he said. 'Course, he always loved to tell a good yarn."

"Good yarn? *Gangster Getaways in the Wisconsin Northwoods.* Izzy, it's perfect!" Shelly reached excitedly for the contest brochure and knocked over her mug, spilling coffee on the ten-year-old letter once again. As the dark liquid dripped over the table edge like another miniwaterfall and down onto the floor, Shelly grabbed a handful of napkins and began to sop it up. "Good things are coming our way, Izzy, I can feel it. Clear skies ahead!"

GIB MURPHY HAD ALWAYS KNOWN the lease would be trouble someday. He'd just hoped to be on the other side of the world when it happened. Well, best-laid plans and all that…

He stepped out of the northern Wisconsin woods onto the sun-drenched beach of Menkesoq Lake, then stopped to let his grandfather and younger brother, Matt, catch up. Like a row of stately blue herons, they fell into a line shoulder to shoulder and looked out across the lake, at a view that had belonged to their family, and the resort they owned, for generations. Though their ages spanned fifty years, all stood straight-backed and tall, but Gib could tell his grandfather's shoulders were starting to round. Hard work and age were taking their toll.

The sun beat down with typical August intensity, heating everything it touched. It was a day meant for riding bikes and climbing trees. A perfect day for swimming and throwing your wet body down on a towel in the hot sand to gaze in wonder at the sky and muse about what it would be like to fly a spaceship.

Too bad he wasn't a kid anymore. Because the subject his grandfather had broached was far too serious for a day like this.

"One hundred years our family's been running this resort, leasing this land from the Gordons," his grandfather said. His silver eyebrows drew together beneath the brim of his worn Chicago Cubs cap. "And now they want to sell it. One hundred years of shared history about to disappear."

Gib could hear the pain in his voice.

"If the land is sold, the improvements become the property of the new owner. That'll be the end of the resort." Matt shielded his blue eyes with his hand as he gazed out over the lake; a breeze ruffled his shaggy brown hair. Though he was twenty, he still had the gangly, not-yet-mature appearance of a teenager.

"Did you talk to them about renegotiating the lease?" Gib asked.

"He tried," Matt said. "They use a management company now."

"Things were easier when we were dealing with Joe Gordon." Their grandfather scooped a couple of sticks from the sand and tossed them into the fieldstone-ringed fire pit. "Once Joe died and his son inherited, well, you know, we haven't seen anyone from that family in twenty years…."

"'Course, they do live in St. Louis. Not exactly down the road," Matt pointed out.

Gib shook his head. Now he remembered why he so seldom came home; every time he did, it seemed like there was some new disaster to contend with. As an Associated Press photojournalist stationed in Iraq, he had enough stress in his life already. "If they're determined to sell, the lease gives you first rights to buy, doesn't it?"

"What it gives us," his grandfather said, "is the right to match any bona fide offer they get."

Gib felt himself relax. "You're okay, then. Nothing to panic about since they haven't even officially put it up for—" Something in his grandfather's expression sent a chill through him. "Tell me they don't already have an offer."

His grandfather grimaced, and for the second time, Gib thought to himself that the man was getting old. Working at the resort kept him reasonably trim, but there were lines around his deep blue eyes that had never been there before.

"Oh, hell! Does this whole thing have to be a game of twenty questions? They got an offer without even listing the property? With six months left on the lease?"

His grandfather nodded. "Some condo developer contacted them. Probably figured it would take six months, anyway, to get all the building plans drawn and approved."

"He gets all his ducks in a row now, then as soon as the lease expires, he's ready to go," Matt said.

"How much time do we have to match the offer?"

His grandfather pressed his lips together. "The lease gives us thirty days but—"

"A month!"

"Actually, there's only twenty-three days left," Matt said.

"Dammit! Did you talk to the bank about getting a loan?"

A long silence greeted his question. He glanced between his brother and grandfather. "Well?"

His grandfather cleared his throat. "Yeah. Yeah, we met with them. They turned us down flat. Gib, we're in trouble. If we can't find a way to buy the land…"

Why did he ever come home? "How's business been?"

"Not what it used to be, that's for sure," Matt said.

"What he means is the old days, when we were full every week all summer, they're gone." His grandfather's shoulders sagged. "I'm thinking a fella may have to pick up some side business to stay afloat."

"Come on!" Gib faced his grandfather. "How many times do I have to tell you? You've gotta stop that. You can't be making book out of the resort—"

"I did quit. But if we need the money—"

"Yeah, well, you won't need the money if you get busted and sent to jail."

"Gib, I only do the small-potatoes stuff—some baseball pools, the local guys, nothing fancy. Your grandmother—"

"Don't try to pretend Grandma ever approved of this. You start bookmaking again and sooner or later you'll get caught and then lose the resort whether you buy the land or not." He looked at his brother. "How can you let him even consider this?"

Matt rolled his eyes. "You think he listens to me?"

"Why don't you threaten to report him or something? Or…threaten to tell Grandma. That would do it—"

"That would not do it," his grandfather said. "It wouldn't make any difference. If it comes to it, I'll do what I have to, to keep this place in our family's name."

The wind shifted and blew a cooler breeze off the lake. *Like an omen,* Gib thought to himself. *And not a good one.* He gritted his teeth together and mentally embraced a picture of what he'd hoped to find once he got home—a relaxing, peaceful environment where he could recuperate from the shrapnel injury he got in Iraq. A chance to purge the memories—

"Kind of a pointless discussion right now, considering the bigger problem," Matt said.

"He's right, Gib. We need to find some money—big money."

Gib went out onto the pier, squinted into the bright afternoon sun as he looked out over the lake, its surface no longer smooth but marred by ripples from the light wind. If they lost the resort, his grandparents and brother had nowhere to live, no way to earn a living. He had no doubt Matt would land on his feet, but his grandparents? They were too old to start over. He turned. "What exactly did the bank say when you met with them? Why'd they say no? I heard Bill Campbell got promoted to vice president in charge of lending a while ago. You should have talked directly to him."

When neither replied, he gazed past them in frustration, up the hill to the main lodge, a large two-story stone-and-log building that was almost a hundred years old. Things were looking a bit neglected and bookings were down; he had more than a sneaking suspicion why they couldn't get the loan.

A blue midsize car bounced along the gravel road and jerked to a stop in front of the lodge. The car's front doors opened and two young women got out. They looked around for a moment, then went up the steps, stopping briefly to pet the family's golden retriever, Rascal, on the veranda. Hopefully these were paying customers and not bill collectors. "Let me guess. The resort is a poor risk because you don't have enough bookings and you don't have enough bookings because the place is getting run-down."

Matt winced and crossed the beach to the water's edge. "Uh, something like that."

"Something," his grandfather echoed.

"Something? What else is there?" Gib retraced his steps down the pier and went to stand beside his brother. The lake lapped at the sand inches from their feet. "They'd rather some developer get the land and put in condos? Like they did on Elk Trail Lake? Like they seem to be doing with all these old resorts?"

Neither answered him.

"They would? Bill actually said—"

"Calm down." Matt shoved his hands in the pockets of his cargo shorts and dug the toe of his running shoe into the sand. "He doesn't want to see condos here. He'd rather see our resort—" Matt slowly blew out his breath. "The problem is, they don't think Grampa or I— Well, you know how business has fallen off. They want some guarantee—"

Gib felt his stomach churn. He was almost afraid to ask. "Guarantee of what?"

"That we'll get it in the black again."

"How are you supposed to do that in twenty-three days?"

"They want us to hire a manager. Thing is, we can't afford—"

Gib waved an arm in front of himself, as much to stop his brother from saying any more as to allow himself to fully focus on their reality. "What are you going to do?" He didn't even want to consider what options might be available. He'd come home to recuperate—not to stay. Running this resort had never been in his plans.

Matt shrugged. "I called the *Wisconsin Getaway Guide* and reminded them we haven't been reviewed in years. Some publicity might help with bookings."

"Hell, Matt, the last time we were in there had to be ten years ago," Gib said. "And if I remember right, we only got three stars then. Now we'd probably only get two. Plus, it'll never be out in time."

Silence settled over them.

"We did okay when you were working here," his grandfather finally said.

No. He'd done his time. He didn't want to do it again. He'd become a freelance photographer to get away, see the world. He had another life, a career. And even though all he wanted to see for the next month was the view of a blue sky from a hammock, he knew he'd eventually take off again, the open road calling him like a siren's song. He slapped a hand against his thigh. "I don't get this manager thing. Grampa, you've been running this place for years. And, Matt, you've been working here practically since you were *two*."

"Bookings are *way* off the past couple of years," his grandfather said. "Bill thinks new blood would bring new ideas."

Gib turned to Matt. "I thought the plan was for you to major in hotel management at the community college during the winters," he said accusingly. "Have you taken any courses yet?"

Matt winced.

"None?" This *so* fit his brother's standard operating behavior. "Maybe if you'd ever get off the ski hill and put some time in around here… People plan their summer vacations when the snow is flying." He knew his irritation was showing. "What a great welcome home. Wow, it's really nice to walk into an ambush."

"It's not an ambush," his grandfather said.

"Yeah? Then why didn't you call me with this news a week ago?"

His grandfather glanced away. "We didn't want to burden you."

"Thought it would be easier to talk in person," Matt said.

"And harder for me to say no?"

"We just thought we'd ask," his grandfather said quietly. "No harm intended. Knew you'd be home for a while and thought you might be able to help."

Gib picked a stone from the sand and hurled it sidearm out onto the lake. It hit the water and droplets scattered outward—like shrapnel. "I'm sorry about what's going on. I don't want you to lose the resort. But what do you want me to do? And in three weeks' time?" He let another stone fly out over the water. "Why don't you call the Gordons and explain the situation. Tell them that no matter what the lease says, thirty days isn't exactly a considerate amount of notice after *one hundred years* of working together."

"You can tell them yourself," his grandfather said. "Their daughter, Elizabeth Gordon, is checking in today."

CHAPTER TWO

HEARING HER NAME, IZZY GRABBED Shelly by the arm and froze inside the line of trees at the edge of the beach. She stared at the brown-haired man who had just been disparaging her family.

"What does *she* want?" he asked, each word laced with bitterness. "Coming to do Daddy's dirty work? Check out the property to make sure they get every penny they can for it?"

He started toward the woods where Izzy and Shelly were hidden. It was clear he didn't have much use for her, and, frankly, if first impressions mattered for anything, she didn't like him much, either. Her palms began to sweat. Nearly six feet tall, broad shoulders, muscled arms, short dark brown hair...and no smile welcoming them to White Bear Lodge. His faded navy blue T-shirt and khaki shorts were wrinkled as if they'd spent months jammed in the bottom of a duffel bag. A jagged red scar crisscrossed his left knee. He looked like the kind of man who did what he wanted, took what he wanted, just exactly whenever he wanted.

Exactly the kind of man she'd never wanted.

Her heart began to pound.

"When she checks in, give Elizabeth Gordon a

personal message for me," the man tossed over his shoulder. Heat rolled through her belly at the way her name slipped over his tongue. "Tell her to take the land and shove it up her rich little ass."

She caught her breath, shocked at the vehemence in his tone. He crossed the sand, favoring his left leg, then stopped the moment he spotted the two of them. He stared at Izzy and she stared back, speechless, caught in the fire of his gray-blue eyes.

After a strained moment, Shelly jumped into the void. "No one is at the main lodge," she said. "Do you work here?"

He narrowed his eyes as though ready to bite out *hell, no,* then jerked a thumb backward toward the two men still standing at the water's edge. "Talk to them." He stalked onto the path leading back to the main lodge and disappeared into the woods.

Izzy swallowed hard and tried to calm her racing pulse, suddenly dreading having to identify herself to this family. All she wanted to do was make a documentary, not get into a war while she was here.

Shelly stepped toward the older gentleman, hand outstretched. "We don't have a reservation, but thought we'd swing by, anyway. Check to see if there's a chance you have any cottages open for the next week."

Izzy tried to keep her shock from registering on her face. They had a reservation; she'd made it herself five minutes after she received the letter telling them their proposal was one of the ten finalists in the Americana Documentary Film Contest.

The man's tanned face creased with his smile. "Welcome to White Bear Lodge. I'm Pete Murphy, the owner. This is my grandson Matt. And, yes, we do have an opening. For a week?"

"Maybe even two," Shelly said. "We're making a documentary."

"You're in the movie business?" Matt asked.

Shelly dipped her head. "Izzy's a director and I am—"

"The star," Izzy said, relieved to have finally found her voice.

"Well, that's a first for us here," Pete said. "Let's go on up and get you checked in."

Twenty minutes later, after a brief conversation about the topic of their movie, they'd completed the paperwork and put the charges on Shelly's MasterCard. Back in the car, Izzy finally let herself relax. "Jeez, Shelly, thanks."

"For what?" Shelly put the car into gear and turned onto the main drive in search of the side road leading to their cottage. "Saving you from having your identity discovered by that gorgeous guy?"

"*Obnoxious* is the word I would use."

"I figured there was no reason he had to know who you were. Not with that attitude. The land sale doesn't have anything to do with you. Who knows how he might try to disrupt our plans if he knew your parents owned the land."

The car bounced through a row of potholes on the gravel drive and Izzy clutched the armrest in one hand and the keys to the cottage in the other. "As soon as we get into our cabin, I'll use the cell phone to cancel our reservation. Thank goodness I never mentioned the movie when I called the first time." She peered out the window and pointed at a narrow dirt road nearly hidden in the woods. "There it is!"

Shelly spun the steering wheel to the left. The force rammed Izzy against the passenger door, and Shelly turned toward her. "Sorry."

"Ack!" Izzy screeched, and pointed at the small, log-sided cottage looming in their path.

Shelly whipped her attention forward and slammed on the brakes. The car jerked to a stop. "Jeez, sorry. The cabin came out of nowhere."

Izzy dropped her head against the headrest. "Why is my heart beating faster here in the Northwoods of Wisconsin than it ever has in the worst rush hour traffic St. Louis has to offer?"

"Must be the fresh pine air. Or, maybe that guy on the beach. You have to admit he was something to behold."

Izzy huffed. "The one with so many nice things to say about me?"

"What do you expect?" Shelly opened her door and stepped outside. "Your parents are about to sell the land out from under them. Probably leave the family homeless, with no way to make a living. By this time next year, the local news stations will be running stories about how the Murphys are living in cardboard boxes on the streets. One of whom is drop-dead gorgeous and cranky because of a sore leg that probably needs some tender loving care." She waggled her fingers. "From me."

Izzy climbed out of the car. "Breathe. And focus."

"I am focused. On B.B. Beautiful Boy." Shelly's gaze landed on the rustic log cottage and her mouth dropped. "Oh, man, check this place out. It's gross. When did you say you were here last?"

Izzy frowned. Cobwebs and dirty windows were not enough to hide the fact that the trim needed a fresh coat of paint and the log exterior needed cleaning. "I was seven or eight. It was the only time I was ever here— right after my grandfather died and my dad inherited the land." She focused her attention on the surrounding landscape. "It may not be obvious to you, but rustic cabins in the woods aren't my parents' thing."

"It's obvious. Thank goodness the main lodge seems to be in reasonable shape or we'd have to change our title to *The Demise of Gangster Getaways in the North-woods of Wisconsin*."

Izzy grabbed two suitcases from the trunk of the car, pushed open the door to the cabin and cringed at the sight. The interior was like a step back in time.

Shelly followed her inside, carefully setting the video-camera case on the chrome-legged, Formica-topped kitchen table. She lowered herself onto the red-vinyl seat of one of the matching chrome chairs. "They've updated some. I'd say this is more like the sixties."

"Good thing we're not here for the ambience...so to speak." Izzy sat on the worn brown couch and felt a loose spring poking her in the rear. Doubt began to cloud her optimism. This place sure didn't look like a vacation getaway for gangsters flush with illegal cash.

"So...now what?" Shelly asked.

Izzy blinked. Now what, indeed? The closest she'd come to making a movie since her college film class six years ago was when she helped out in the video-editing suite at the station. Her stomach took a nervous flop. It had seemed like a brilliant idea—come out to Wiscon-sin, to the land her family had owned for a hundred years, to the resort that was reputed to have been a summer destination of Prohibition-era Chicago gangsters—and make a documentary. Still photos and maps juxtaposed with new live footage, old letters and newspaper articles dramatically read aloud, short interviews with people who had stories to tell of that time and, beneath everything, the music of the twenties and thirties to evoke the atmosphere of the era. Nothing to it. Just like Ken Burns.

Or not. Ken had hours and hours to tell his story—they would have six minutes. Ken had a full staff, multiple cameras and tons of money. They had her, Shelly, one camera and a few bucks in savings. Her stomach clutched in panic. *What had she been thinking?*

"I can feel it now," Shelly said. "First place in the Americana Documentary Film Contest. And our future all but secured in the film industry."

Izzy snorted. "Keep dreaming."

"It's important to visualize ourselves where we want to be. Use the energy of the universe and the power of your mind to make success happen."

"Don't you feel the least bit nervous about us being able to make the movie, let alone win?"

"Not if we stay focused on putting out positive psychic energy. Besides, we only have ten competitors. And they're like us—amateurs and students—not professional filmmakers." Shelly stretched her shoulders. "Even if we fail, at least you can go to your class reunion having fulfilled your high school dream. For a brief shining moment, you will have been a director."

"That's what I thought when we started this. But once we became finalists, suddenly it feels way more serious."

"Breathe. And focus," Shelly said. "All we're doing right now is getting as much preliminary footage as we can."

"Right." Izzy jumped to her feet, wrestled her video camera from its case and headed for the door. "Come on, the light is perfect right now—let's do some un-scripted filming to get in the mood."

Outside, Shelly jangled the old bell hanging next to the door, then cut across the scrawny patch of grass in front of the cabin. She waved a hand at the triangle of blue sky visible through the green-leafed treetops. "Overhead we have some high cumulus clouds," she said. "A fine summer afternoon with temperatures expected to be around seventy-eight degrees, but—"

"Wrong topic. Remember, you're a star this week, not a weather girl."

"I'm warming up my vocal cords." Shelly displayed her perfect on-air smile and a flawless set of pearly whites. "Could be some cumulonimbus on the horizon. That could mean a repeat of the past few days—with rain in the forecast later on if the wind holds—"

Izzy shut off the camera. "Maybe we should scratch our original subject and do a weather documentary instead."

"People *do* love to talk about the weather."

"Wait, I'm visualizing something… *Last place.* Allow me." Izzy handed the camera to her friend, then picked up a broken signpost on which the cottage name, Beechwood, was visible in faded black paint. She grinned playfully. "Something like this. Long ago, White Bear Lodge was a favorite vacation destination for gangsters like John Dillinger and Al Capone. Now all that remains of their fancy digs is this broken—"

At the sound of a car crunching down the gravel road, she turned to see an old tan Taurus slowly round the corner and pull in alongside their Dodge.

"Beautiful Boy," Shelly whispered when it was clear the driver was the guy from the beach. "Come to visit already." She flexed her fingers.

Izzy's heart started to patter.

Beautiful Boy rested his left arm on the open window. His eyes locked on Izzy and the signpost she was holding. "You ladies have an accident?"

The blood rushed into her face, making her feel flush. She tightened her grip on the wood post and tried to make her mind work.

"Breathe and focus," Shelly muttered.

"We found this on the ground…someone else must have broken it." She knew she sounded like she was lying.

"Are you a guest here at White Bear?" Shelly asked.

Leave it to Shelly to get right to the heart of things.

"I…uh, sort of."

He wasn't one of the owners? Then why had he gone on that rant about her?

Shelly stepped closer to the car. "Have you been here before?"

He let out a sharp laugh. "Oh, yeah. Been coming here for years." He lowered the volume on the radio. "Listen, I'm heading into town. My grandmother asked me to tell you dinner tonight is down at the beach—a cookout from four-thirty to six-thirty."

"So you're not a guest?" Izzy couldn't help asking.

"I wish it were that simple," he muttered. "No, I'm Gib Murphy. Back for a visit." He glanced from Izzy to

Shelly and back again, gray eyes locking with Izzy's just long to make her squirm inside. "And you are?"

She almost gulped. "Izzy. Izzy Stuart," she lied, giving her first and middle names only. No way was she going to let on that she was Elizabeth Gordon. "And this is Shelly Kent."

"Nice to meet you, ladies. I'll save some marshmallows for you at the fire pit." He put the car into gear. "If you need anything during your stay, be sure to let me know."

As he drove away, Shelly fanned herself. "Need anything? My Lord," she said, "yes, there is something I'm needing. Sad to say, but it's not me he's wanting it from. Did you see the way he looked at you?"

Izzy stared after the car, still feeling as disconcerted as she had when Gib's gaze was on her. "He didn't look at me like anything. Unless he's figured out my family owns the land."

"Land?" Shelly barked out a laugh. "Those eyes had nothing to do with land, honey. Unless, that is, you're lying flat on your back on it."

"ULTRAMODERN CABINS? An unparalleled vacation experience?" Bill Campbell, the bank vice president, handed the yellowed trifold White Bear Lodge brochure back to Gib and picked up his pruning shears. Though he was only in his mid-forties, Bill's dark hair showed far more salt than pepper and there was no hiding the extra weight he'd put on around the middle. He had the appearance of a content, middle-aged man. "You know as well as I do the place hasn't been updated since it was built."

"That's not exactly true—"

"Updates in the sixties don't count." Bill trimmed the wayward branches on an overgrown lilac bush.

Gib winced. There was no way he could argue otherwise. He stepped into a patch of shade and contemplated the Campbell's beautifully landscaped backyard. What had he been thinking, impulsively coming here on a Saturday afternoon when all he'd planned to do in town was pick up marshmallows and chocolate bars for tonight's cookout? "Bill, you've been friends with our family a long time. I know my grampa is getting tired. And Matt's hardly more than a kid. But can't you lend them the money on the condition that Matt takes some management classes at the local college?"

"They need more help than Matt's going to get in a few classes. Plus, they need promotion. A Web site. A new brochure—not that thing written forty years ago—"

"Not to mention a fresh coat of paint," Gib muttered.

"Right. You see it. That's the insight that would come with new management. A fresh approach to things." He dropped a handful of cut branches on the ground.

Gib scooped them up and tossed them into a nearby trash can filled with other yard debris. "Classes in hotel and restaurant management could teach Matt some of that stuff," he pressed.

"No time. There's only a few weeks. I can't gamble *now* that classes would help Matt figure out how to run the place *later.*"

Gib squeezed the fingers of one hand into a fist. "If you lent them the money and they defaulted on the payments, the bank would get the land. That's valuable property. It's win-win for the bank no matter what you do."

"Gib, we're in the business of lending money—not the business of buying and selling property. We don't make loans just to take property back."

Yeah. He knew that.

Bill began to trim another bush. "Face it. Your grand-father's getting old. Your brother is awfully young, and, frankly, I don't think his heart is in it, anyway."

"They can't hire a manager. They can hardly afford to pay the part-time help they have right now."

"I'm sorry, Gib. I hope this doesn't sound heartless, but maybe it would be best for everyone if the land was sold and all of you moved on to the next chapter of your lives."

That would be fine if his grandparents had any money in the bank, if they had any way to support them-selves once they left the property *if they were interested in leaving.* But they weren't. As much as he wanted to agree with Bill, he wouldn't be able to live with himself if he walked away and let them lose everything. "It's not that simple. If the land is sold, the buildings go with it. So the next chapter for Matt and my grandparents means having nowhere to live. And no means of making a living. Come on, Bill, you've known my family forever. Lend them the money. Isn't there some *outside the box* thing you could do?"

Bill straightened, thinking. "Outside the box, huh? They need a manager, someone who can see the big picture, then break it down into the sum of its parts and make it work again." He gestured across his backyard. "This place was a jungle when we moved in. Look at it now. That's what White Bear needs. Vision. And a plan."

Gib's spirits dropped. Matt's vision was limited to anything that had to do with skiing. And his grandfather…well, he'd said it before, his grandfather was tired.

"Hey, here's an idea outside the box—why don't you do it? The place did all right when you were still at home. Wasn't breaking any sales records, but it ran in the black."

No. Not him. He couldn't go back, not to the resort, not to being tied down 24/7 and dealing with guests all the time. He pictured Izzy Stuart standing beside the cottage with that broken signpost in her hands, her long brown hair mussed from the wind, brown eyes sparkling, cheeks pink with embarrassment. He frowned. Even the most appealing of guests created stress.

"With all due respect, what else were you planning to do?"

"I was planning to take some time off," Gib said, holding his temper in check. "Then I'll go back to photojournalism. A bum knee doesn't mean I can't push a camera button anymore."

Bill tossed some cut branches on the ground, but didn't answer. After a beat, Gib said, "So, that's it? If I become the manager, you'll approve the loan?" Even though all he was doing was asking, he felt he'd stepped into quicksand.

"Well, getting more bookings and breaking even would help, too."

"There's only twenty-three days left. It's not going to happen that fast. Besides, it's August. Most of the world has either taken their summer vacations or has them already planned."

Bill closed the pruning shears and faced Gib. "We're in one of the worst financial markets in history. Loans are going into default everywhere, and the bank—like every bank—has substantially tightened its lending guidelines. I'd love to help you out, but in this market, if you want a loan, you have to bend over backward. Prove to the loan committee you're going to make White Bear Lodge viable again."

Reality sank slowly into Gib's brain. "Just in case we don't manage to get a lot of new bookings in the next three weeks, do you have any suggestions for plan B?"

"It might help your case if we knew the resort was making strides—big ones—in the right direction." Bill opened and shut the clippers a couple of times as he spoke. "Competent management, a Web site, new brochure. Upgrade one of the cottages to show how you plan to renovate all of them."

Gib raked a hand through his hair. He must be crazy to even consider this. But he was going to be home for a while, anyway. And if he didn't try to help… "Okay, I'll do it. I'll manage the place." *For a while.* "We'll put together a plan, work on bookings, develop a Web site, make a new brochure, renovate a cottage." *How the hell was he going to pull all this off in three weeks?* "Then you'll lend them the money?"

Bill dropped his shears on the ground and pulled off his gloves. "I can't promise anything. But a good-faith effort can't hurt when the loan committee reviews your request."

IZZY BEGAN TO METHODICALLY empty her suitcase into the old wooden dresser in the bedroom she'd be using for the next week or two. Socks and underwear in the first drawer, tops in the second, shorts in the third—

"I have never in my life understood why people unpack on vacation," Shelly said from the doorway. She threw herself onto the garish orange-flowered spread covering the double bed and propped her chin in her hands. "All it does is create more work when you have to repack to leave."

"It feels more like a real escape when you unpack," Izzy said. "Like you've actually gone away for an extended holiday."

"Sounds like something your parents or Andrew would say. *No well-bred person would live out of a suitcase.* Speaking of your betrothed, did you call him yet to say we arrived?"

Izzy stopped, three brightly colored T-shirts in her hands. "He's not my betrothed."

"Someone better tell him."

She stuck the shirts in the drawer and closed it firmly. "I was doing nicely here, not even thinking about Andrew, and then you had to bring him up."

"Well. Now, that sounds like true love speaking. I bet fifty bucks you never marry him."

Izzy lined up her Adidas and sandals on the closet floor. "Okay, you're on. I may be having some trouble getting past that little surprise he sprang on me at the airport, but that doesn't mean we won't spend our lives together."

"You mean that oh-so-romantic proposal?" Shelly laughed.

"That would be it." Izzy lifted a black dress out of her bag, shook out the wrinkles and hung it in her closet.

"Where in the Wisconsin woods are you planning to wear *that?*"

"You should always pack a little black dress. Then, no matter what comes up, you're ready."

Shelly's mouth dropped open. "If I wanted to be here making a documentary with Andrew, I would have asked him along."

"I didn't bring it because of him."

"No, no, absolutely not."

Izzy put her toiletries kit on top of the dresser and unzipped the case, carefully setting out her travel-size Chanel No.5 and the goat-milk hand cream Andrew had given her. Sometimes she wondered what was so wrong with Curel lotion. She pushed the troubling thought away.

Shelly rolled onto her back and laced her hands behind her head. "What I don't get is, if you said *no,* how come he acted like you said *yes?*"

Izzy pressed her lips together. She'd glossed over the details when she'd told Shelly the story on the plane. "That's just Andrew. He kind of turned it into *yes.*"

"How does *no* kind of turn into *yes?*"

"Well, I actually never said *no.* What I said was, I would think about it."

"What?" Shelly sat up.

"I just wanted to get on the plane without a big discussion. If I'd said no, well, imagine how awful that could have been." She deposited her hair dryer and the rest of her toiletries in the bathroom.

"You could have said no and still gotten on the plane without a big discussion. *No, I'm not ready yet* would have let him down gently right on the spot."

"Yeah… But he said he'd checked the June availability at the country club and found an open date…and that June, you know, is the perfect wedding month. So I didn't want—"

"You can't be going along with this!"

Izzy winced. "He just likes to be organized. And, well, really, what's not to like about marrying Andrew Clarkson? He's—"

"Well dressed, attractive, gainfully employed, has a full head of hair. In a word, perfect. The kind of man your parents consider a great catch."

"The kind of man most women consider a great catch." A picture of Gib Murphy stole into Izzy's head, his gray, dangerous eyes boring into hers. A wave of heat rushed through her and she sat on the edge of the bed. "The kind of man most women want to settle down with," she said in an attempt to force Gib out of her thoughts. She let herself fall backward onto the bed so she could stare at the ceiling, feet still on the floor. Gib Murphy and his wrinkled T-shirt and broad chest and strong arms and muscled legs and even that angry scar on his knee—all of it, *all of him* filled her mind. "He's absolutely perfect," she whispered.

Problem was, she was no longer talking about Andrew.

CHAPTER THREE

"WHAT TOOK YOU SO LONG?" Matt stood on a tall stool and rummaged through the cupboard above the refrigerator where the liquor was usually kept.

Gib dropped the grocery bag of marshmallows and chocolate bars on the kitchen counter. His family didn't even know he'd gone to talk to Bill Campbell, let alone that he'd agreed to take the manager's job. Now he wasn't quite sure how to tell them.

"What are you doing?"

"We can't find the hot dog and marshmallow skewers," his grandmother said as she hurried through the doorway, a bundle of energy for such a tiny woman. She was a little more plump than the last time he'd been home, and a little more frazzled. She put a hand on each side of her head, smashing her gray curls and framing her softly lined face. "They're not in the storage room anywhere. I swear, we get more disorganized every year. Maybe it *is* time to retire."

"You think?" Matt leaned over to open another of the high cupboard doors.

"Didn't we always keep them with all the rest of the barbecue utensils?" Gib asked.

His grandmother clucked her tongue as she pulled a

chef's apron from a drawer and put it on. "Usually. But they're not there."

"You know what they say about *usually*," Matt said.

"The welcome cookout last week, a huge storm came in. I swear, it was like *The Wizard of Oz*." His grandmother dug through a drawer. "Total chaos getting everything off the beach. We were running around like chickens with their heads cut off. The guests were helping carry things up and now we can't find anything."

"What *do* they say about *usually?*" Gib asked, struggling to follow the threads of the conversation.

"I don't know. But I'm sure they say something. Here they are!" Matt climbed down from the stool brandishing the skewers. He handed one to Gib. *"En garde!"* He struck an exaggerated fencing pose and Gib did the same.

The two dueled their way around the kitchen like they had many a time as kids. Gib backed Matt up against the big stainless-steel refrigerator. "Uncle. Say *uncle*," he said.

"Boys!" Their grandmother clapped her hands firmly. "We have a cookout in an hour and we're not nearly ready!"

"Uncle." Gib ignored her.

"Never." Matt grinned.

"Boys!"

Gib took a step back and handed his skewer to his brother. "This isn't over. Don't ever think you'll get the better of *the resort master.*"

"You can only be resort master if you're part of the resort." Matt stuck the skewers in the cardboard box on the table, then added the bag of groceries Gib had picked up.

"I *am* part of the resort. That's what took me so long in town."

Matt squinted. "What does that mean?"

"I talked to Bill Campbell." He watched Matt's face closely, waiting to see the realization hit him.

Their grandmother turned, her arms laden with disposable plastic cups and paper plates. "You talked to Bill? Where? It's Saturday."

"At his house. I tried to get him to give you guys the loan. And he agreed—"

"He agreed?" Matt sounded stunned.

The paper plates and plastic cups clattered to the worn linoleum floor. "He agreed?" His grandmother's voice was hardly more than a whisper.

Gib bent to help her gather everything up. "It's more complicated than that." He explained the agreement he'd made with Bill. "Still no guarantee of the loan, but it's a step in the right direction."

"Wow," Matt said, not sounding very excited.

"That is a *wow*," his grandmother said. "Honey, you've been through a lot already. If you don't want to run the resort, you shouldn't feel like you have to."

Matt pulled a can of Mountain Dew from the refrigerator and popped it open. "I don't get it. This morning you were like, *no way*. What changed?"

Gib blinked. This wasn't the reaction he'd expected at all. "Don't everyone jump with joy at once."

"Oh, we're happy." Matt threw a roll of paper towel and a package of napkins into the box. "Grampa's going to be really happy."

"He's right. Your grampa will be thrilled." Grandma bobbed her head.

Gib hoped his grandfather showed it more than these two. "Well, if that's the case, I think I'll go find him right now." He held himself back from adding, *Because it would be nice to talk to someone who is honestly thrilled over the news.* "Where is Grampa, anyway?"

"He drove a load of firewood to the beach," Matt said.

"I'll take this stuff down there and fill him in." Gib lifted the box from the table and headed out the door. He didn't get it. If he didn't know better, he'd think his decision to become the resort manager had just ruined his brother's day.

The dog followed him off the porch and down to the beach. "At least you seem happy about it, Rascal."

Gib dropped the box on a picnic table and went to help his grandfather unload wood from the back of the golf cart. He was surprised at how empty the beach was; the only people there were an elderly couple, Mr. and Mrs. Steinmetz, sitting in lawn chairs near the water's edge. They'd been regulars at White Bear every summer for forty years. "Where is everyone?" he asked his grandfather.

"Late enough in the afternoon that most folks are done swimming by now."

"Kids aren't. They'll swim no matter what the time or temperature."

"Like I told you before, bookings are down," the older man said. "Something's wrong, but darned if I know what. It's not like we've changed anything… The bank'd probably say that's what the problem is."

"That's what they did say." Gib piled an armload of wood next to the fire pit and told his grandfather about his decision.

Pete helped stack the wood, then pulled off his baseball cap and wiped his forehead with the back of his hand. "Well, Gib, I'm proud of you. Thanks for going to see him. Looks like we've got our work cut out for us if we're going to hang on to this place."

Gib stared at him in confusion. Once again, no excitement.

"What's going on? Everyone's reacting to this news sort of like, *that's nice*. This morning you guys were practically begging me to become the manager. Now that I agreed, it feels like no one cares. If none of you want to save the place, why should I?"

"Everyone cares, Gib," his grandfather said quietly. "The three of us have spent the past week chasing down every idea we could think of to get the money. Not one was successful." He climbed into the golf cart driver's seat. "You can't blame us for not letting our hopes go too high."

Gib took the seat next to him, not sure what to say in response to the sobering reality of his grandparents' situation.

An hour later, the whole thing was gone from his mind. The cookout was in full swing and Gib was too busy to put much thought into his family's reaction to his decision to stay. He opened a can of Dr. Pepper and considered the small group of people who had gathered to roast hot dogs around the open fire. The smell of burning wood hovered in the air, making it feel like an autumn night even though cooler weather was still a month away. If this was the sum total of the week's guests, the resort was in even worse shape than he'd thought. He leaned close to his grandmother. "Is this it for guests?"

"Prit-near." The corners of her mouth turned down. "We're in trouble, Gib. Don't know if it can be fixed even with you at the helm."

He patted her shoulder, wanting only to see the strain leave her face. "Where there's a will, there's a way," he said with more confidence than he felt. If his grandparents and brother didn't want to stay here so badly, he'd have been the first to stand up and argue the resort should be sold. But they did. The place needed saving, and since the bank thought he was the only person to do it, he'd give it the best he had.

His grandfather stood to address the assembled guests and held up a skewer with a flaming marshmallow at the end like a torch. "Welcome to White Bear Lodge," he said. "I'm Pete Murphy, the owner. This is my wife, Catherine. Many of you have been here before, some are new. Since we're all gonna be neighbors for the next week or two, let's go around and give our names." He blew out the fire on the marshmallow and gestured with the charred lump. "If you're feeling talkative, tell us something about yourself. And if you're not, don't."

A log in the fire cracked and sent sparks flying. Pete waved the skewer again. "I'll go first. Like I said, I'm Pete Murphy. That golden retriever you see running around here is mine—name's Rascal. I've been running White Bear Lodge for near forty-five years—took over from my dad in the sixties. My grandfather started this resort back in 1910 at the ripe old age of twenty-four…."

As Pete launched into White Bear's history, Gib let his thoughts slip away. There had always been an unspoken expectation that White Bear Lodge would pass from generation to generation. But Gib's dad had never wanted to stay; he'd always needed more than the resort offered—more excitement, more challenge, more freedom.

He glanced up as his grandmother began her introduction. For the first time in his life, he wondered what it had felt like when her only child, Gib's dad, had taken off to see the world, for years his only contact with home an occasional phone call and the postcards he sent from all over the planet. Had it hurt to learn of his marriage weeks after it happened? To not meet his wife until almost two years later?

Matt nudged his shoulder. "Your turn."

Gib stood and held up his soda. "I'm Gib Murphy, Pete's grandson. I'm a photojournalist for the Associated Press. Just finished an assignment and thought I'd come home for some R and R. Which I suspect I'm not going to get. I've been back two days and they're already making plans to work me to the bone."

Everyone chuckled and Gib dropped into his lawn chair again. That was as much detail as they needed. He didn't want to deal with the questions that inevitably came whenever people learned he'd been in Iraq.

He tried to pay attention as the guests introduced themselves, but was instantly distracted when Izzy and Shelly joined the group late, taking the lawn chairs directly opposite him. Izzy skewered a hot dog and stuck it directly into the flames, pulling it out minutes later, fully charbroiled. She made a face at her blackened dinner, then gamely wrapped the dog in a bun, smothered it in enough condiments to kill the taste and took a bite. A glob of relish dripped onto her lower lip and she licked it off. He looked away, wondering if she had a boyfriend and whether it bothered the guy that she was off in the woods without him. And then he wondered why he cared.

Finally only Shelly and Izzy were left to speak. Izzy stood first, gracefully unfolding from her chair. She self-consciously reached up and played with a strand of her long brown hair. "I'm Izzy Stuart," she said. "I'm here to vacation and to, um, make a documentary."

Gib slowly straightened in his lawn chair.

"My friend Shelly and I are making a movie about the vacations Chicago gangsters took in Wisconsin during the twenties and thirties. The talk is, they liked to stay at several resorts in the area, including White Bear Lodge."

A movie? They were planning to film at White Bear? What a stroke of luck. This could be great for business. Free publicity to get their name out, build a reputation, show people the resort. *Show people the resort?*

Damn. This could be terrible for business.

No one would be impressed by White Bear in its present condition—no matter who stayed here in the twenties. If this movie got any distribution, it could be the kiss of death for turning things around. He tried to catch his grandfather's eye, but the older man was grinning broadly at Izzy.

"A real movie?" Gib asked, hoping to hear it was nothing more than an assignment for some college class. "When will it be released?"

"It probably won't be released," Izzy said. "We're finalists in the Americana Documentary Film Contest, so the only people who will see it are the judges. Besides, it'll only be six minutes long."

Gib started to relax.

"Unless we win," Shelly said. "Then who knows? Anything could happen. Maybe we'll end up on YouTube." She stood and quickly introduced herself to the group.

As soon as she finished speaking, his grandfather stepped forward and brought his hands together with a clap. "That covers everyone who's here tonight. Feel free to hang around as long as you like. If you need something, let one of us know. We got all the fixings for s'mores so no one goes back to their cottage till the chocolate bars are gone!"

Gib wandered over next to his grandfather and steered him farther down the beach. "Did you hear that? They're making a movie," he murmured.

Pete nodded. "Neat, huh?"

"Yeah, except we're a little run-down around here."

"The movie's not about the resort."

"Sure it is." Gib glanced at the old boathouse sadly in need of a coat of paint. "They'll be filming the lodge and cottages. Gangster history or not, that's all anyone would have to see to know this is the last place they want to stay on a vacation."

"Any publicity is good publicity. Isn't that what they say?"

"*They* don't know everything."

"Excuse me, Pete?"

Gib turned.

Izzy stood a few steps away, watching his grandfather expectantly. "We were wondering if you have time tomorrow to share the stories your father used to tell. Maybe even get some of it on film." She smiled, and he could see his grandfather turning to mush under her gaze. Obviously, the man didn't have it in him to say no to a pretty woman. Well, Gib didn't have that problem.

"Uh, Izzy, it's flattering that you want to make a movie here. But you can't shoot on private property without getting permission from the owners."

She drew her brows together and lifted her eyes to his. "I got permission."

"From who?"

Pete cleared his throat. "Me."

"Signed a release form, too," Shelly said as she came up to them.

"You might have mentioned it," he said to his grandfather, trying not to sound strained.

"Is there a problem?" Izzy asked.

A tall, thin man in a polo shirt and khakis stepped across the beach toward them. "Sorry I'm so late, Pete. You have time to, ah, talk about that—"

"Yup, let's run up to the lodge," his grandfather said. "Ladies, if you'll excuse me, I've got a quick bit of business to take care of, then I'll be right back."

Gib stared at the two men as they walked away. This better not be side business. His grandfather would end up in jail someday if he wasn't careful. He turned his attention back to Izzy. "Problem?" he echoed. No, there wasn't a problem. With everything going on around here, the word was *problems. Plural.* On top of creating a Web site, redoing the brochure, renovating one of the cottages and keeping his grandfather from getting back into bookmaking, he now had to make sure Izzy Stuart's documentary showed White Bear in the best possible light so it didn't end up biting them in the butt. "No problem at all. Let me know if I can be of any help."

"I'M CHANGING MY MIND about how hot that Gib guy is," Shelly said as she and Izzy walked through the woods to their cottage. Though the moon was nearly full, they still needed a flashlight to illuminate the path. "I don't think he was very happy about our filming here. I was watching him when you first started talking and I thought he was going to have a coronary."

"Beautiful Boy? He looked normal to me."

Shelly shook her head. "That's because you can't get past that face. That body. That mouth. That— Well, we won't go there. Those of us less invested in superficial—"

A laugh burst out of Izzy. It was pretty hard not to notice Gib Murphy. "Right. That would be you."

"Like I was saying, we notice other, more subtle things. And that man would have keeled over right then and there if he'd had any blockage in his arteries to help the process along. But since he didn't, he simply dragged his grandfather to the other end of the beach to discuss the issue."

"He didn't drag him to the other end of the beach."

"Regardless, he wasn't happy about us filming here."

"Maybe it just caught him by surprise." As she unlocked the door to their cottage, she heard her cell phone inside begin sounding its traditional telephone-bell ring tone. Andrew felt it showed a lack of class to use any other type of ring. "No need to draw attention to yourself like that," he always said. "Phones should alert the owner, not put on a stage show."

She recognized his number on the ID and flipped opened her phone to answer.

"Elizabeth," Andrew said before she even had a chance to say hello. "I've been doing some thinking about this documentary."

"Hello, Andrew." She took an ice cream bar from the freezer and peeled off the wrapper.

"You know I support you completely."

"Yes." She bit into the frozen chocolate, not really believing him, but not in the mood to get into a disagreement.

"But I've been having second thoughts."

She tightened her grip on the phone. "You just said you supported me."

"I do. But some things are more important than this movie—"

"Like what?"

"Like our family?"

She sucked in a breath. "Mine or yours?"

"Ours, honey. The family we're going to have."

"I'm concentrating on making a documentary right now—not having a family. My new career—"

"That's my other point. *What new career?* I mean, if we're getting married next June, working in the film industry isn't realistically in your future. At least not for very long."

"And why not?" She took another bite of ice cream.

"Well, sweetheart." His voice took on a patronizing edge. "Because, before long you'll be thirty. Your eggs are getting older. You know how we've always talked about having a baby three years after the wedding."

How you've always talked about having a baby three years after the wedding, she thought. Like life was this thing that could be planned out day to day, years in advance. "Sometimes it doesn't work that easily."

"All the more reason not to postpone too long because of a career."

She shoved more ice cream into her mouth. "Andrew, is this why you called? To talk about starting a family in three years?"

"Well, yes. That and the movie." He paused. "Are you eating on the phone?"

"Ice cream."

"Oh."

Funny how so much disapproval could be expressed in one syllable. For a moment she wished she had potato chips she could chomp.

"My point is, I've never heard you mention wanting to make movies before. So why put all this time and effort, not to mention money, into making a documentary when—"

"Because at least we'll have made the movie," she said defensively. She threw her licked-clean stick in the trash and took the second ice cream bar Shelly held out to her.

"Yes, but—"

"And at least I'll be able to go to my class reunion having fulfilled my dreams in the smallest way. I thought you understood that."

"I do. But there's more to think about than simply what *you* want."

Izzy clenched her teeth together. "Andrew. I'm making this documentary."

A long empty silence answered her. Andrew cleared his throat. "I'm just saying that there are more things to take into consideration now than there might have been even a few weeks ago."

"I can't believe we're even having this conversation." She locked eyes with Shelly and gave her head a shake. Ice cream dripped onto the back of her hand and she licked it off, feeling a small, selfish satisfaction that Andrew would flip if he saw her do that.

"I'm just asking you to reconsider," he said.

"I have to go. Shelly's calling me from outside," she lied.

"Tell me you'll at least think about what I'm saying."

"Fine. I'll think about it. I have to go." She closed her phone before he could say anything else, realizing only then that she hadn't said goodbye.

She'd never hung up on Andrew before in her life.

CHAPTER FOUR

EARLY THE NEXT MORNING, GIB HEADED to the kitchen for breakfast duty. A gentle breeze rippled the flags in front of the main lodge, and carried with it the scents of pine and wildflowers. He yawned, his fatigue so great he felt like he'd been trampled by a bull—7:30 a.m. was for sleeping. Or running. Except both activities had been a problem since his injury.

He switched his thoughts to the discussion he planned to have with Izzy and Shelly today. By providing them with some information—as little as possible—he hoped to convince them to minimize the footage they used of the resort. As long as they kept their camera on the areas that were still in decent shape, the place might come off all right on film. Especially if it was in the background…and soft focus. "Okay, I'm here," he announced as he came through the door. "What do you want me to do today?"

His grandmother pulled a jug of milk from the refrigerator and set it on the center island. "Wait tables," she said.

"Again? Maybe I could cook."

"Got plenty of cooks today—your brother and I are already taking care of that. Grampa ran into town and he's not back yet, so we need you to wait tables. There's waitstaff aprons in the—"

"I know where they are." He went out into the hall and grabbed a black apron and order pad from the top drawer of an antique buffet. Waiting tables was one of the reasons he'd gone to college. So he wouldn't get stuck running White Bear, being *the help,* for the rest of his life.

And here he was again.

Although, he reminded himself, this was a temporary gig, not the rest of his life.

"The dining room opens at eight, so go ahead and check the sugar bowls, salt and peppers, get out the—"

"I remember the drill." Oh, how well he remembered the drill.

By eight-thirty, more than twenty people were breakfasting in the spacious stone-and-log-walled dining room. The decor hadn't changed much since the lodge was built; that was one of its most appealing aspects. Its stone walls and dark woods made the building cozy and comfortable. From above the fireplace, a deer head with a set of ten-point antlers stood watch. The other walls were adorned with fishing poles, canoe paddles and wildlife paintings.

Gib picked up a pot of fresh-brewed coffee and began to refill cups as he made his way to where Izzy and Shelly were seated at a small round table near the windows overlooking the veranda. As he neared, Izzy tilted her head and a beautiful smile opened her face. Her hair was pulled back in a ponytail and she wore no makeup, and yet his first thought was that he wanted to touch her. Touch her and then kiss her.

He shook off the thought. "Morning, ladies. Coffee?"

At their eager nods, he filled the white ceramic mugs with steaming liquid. "Did you sleep well last night?"

"Like a log in the woods." Shelly doctored her coffee with generous amounts of cream and sugar.

"Me, too," Izzy said.

"And you? How did you sleep last night?" Shelly asked.

He hesitated, remembering how he'd awakened drenched in sweat, reliving in his dreams the nightmare he'd survived in Iraq several months ago. Not sleeping well had become the norm for him. "Really well."

Izzy raised her eyebrows.

"You don't believe me?"

"You've got that *I've been up half the night* face," she said.

He shrugged. Awfully perceptive, that one.

"Still extremely handsome," Shelly hastily added.

"That's all that matters." He could tell Izzy was watching him, wondering, and he put on the friendly host face he'd perfected as a teenager. No way was he going to elaborate on his problems. "Can I interest you in something to eat? We've got quite a selection this morning, beginning with the country breakfast—scrambled eggs, bacon and sausage, hash browns, toast. Or omelets made to order. Or—" He gestured at a long table nearby. "There are doughnuts, bagels, homemade muffins, yogurt and an assortment of cereals. I think you'll find that one thing you'll never be at White Bear Lodge is hungry."

"Or thin," Shelly added. "The camera adds ten pounds, so if I add ten of my own these next couple of weeks, won't I be a lovely sight in the documentary?"

"You can always ditch the movie. Then your weight won't be an issue," he said.

The two women laughed.

"Did I miss something?"

"No," Izzy said. "Nothing worth knowing."

"Well, to combat your concerns, let me suggest the yogurt and granola. And my grandmother does run a water aerobics class in the lake Tuesday and Thursday mornings at eleven."

Shelly pretended to weigh her options in either hand. "Big breakfast. Yogurt and granola. Lose ten pounds. Gain ten pounds. Hmm. Even though this feels like a vacation, I should probably control myself." She ran a finger down the menu. "Okay, two eggs sunny-side up, sausage, hash browns, whole wheat toast. And—"

"That is an admirable amount of control," Izzy deadpanned.

"Add in a couple of pancakes. And a large orange juice. All this fresh air is making me work up an appetite." Shelly pointed a finger at Izzy. "We'll start over tomorrow."

Gib wrote everything down. "Anything else?"

"I think the better question is, is there anything left in the kitchen?" Izzy asked. "I'll have a Swiss cheese and mushroom omelet, whole wheat toast and orange juice."

A few minutes later, Gib returned with the orange juice, intent on beginning a discussion about their filming at the resort. "When do you start shooting the documentary?"

"This afternoon." Izzy sipped her coffee. "We're going to interview your grandfather."

A shriek came from the direction of the kitchen and

Gib turned toward the double doors just as a loud curse from his brother echoed through the room. "Excuse me." He sprinted across the hardwood floor and burst into the kitchen. Flames billowed from an oversize pan on the stove and lapped at an adjacent cupboard. His grandmother flailed a wet towel at the fire like a trapped bird flapping its wings in a small space, while his brother shot fire extinguisher powder on everything in the immediate area. Each was shouting unheeded instructions at the other.

A flash of memory shot into his mind—the explosion he'd survived. He rammed the thought away and grabbed his grandmother's arm. "Get the hell back before you get hurt. Lower, Matt, aim at the base of the fire. Not the flames. All you're doing is spreading it. *Lower, Matt!* Shoot right into the pan!"

When the flames finally subsided, he looked closely at his grandmother. "Are you okay? Did you call the fire department?"

The wail of a siren and then another and yet a third answered his question. A three-alarm fire? "Welcome to Grand Central Station," he muttered. "Nothing like small-town boredom to light a fire under everyone. Literally."

Though the flames were out, Matt shot another stream of powder into the general area, apparently for good measure. "Holy crap. I only looked away for a minute," he said.

"That's all it ever takes," Grandma said.

Sirens screaming, the trucks stopped in front of the lodge, the high-pitched squeal almost surreal in the Wisconsin woods. Gib touched his brother on the shoulder. "I'll go settle down the guests, you deal with the firefighters."

Out in the dining hall he quickly explained the situation with the grease fire. "Everything is fine. Nothing to worry about. Except…there's one problem… The grill is out of commission for at least the rest of the morning—there's fire extinguisher powder on everything. So help yourselves to our continental selection. Bagels, toast, fruit, yogurt…" He gestured toward the well-stocked table. "Hopefully, tomorrow's breakfast will be less eventful."

He answered a couple of questions then cut diagonally through the room to Izzy and Shelly's table. "Sorry to be the bearer of bad news, but your big breakfasts will have to be another day." Though he knew he should get back into the kitchen, he didn't want to lose this chance to talk to the girls about limiting the amount of filming they did at White Bear. He hesitated, not sure how to broach the subject. Finally he just dove in. "When you begin filming this afternoon, would you keep something in mind?"

Izzy's brows pulled together in confusion.

"I would guess you've noticed that White Bear is looking somewhat…"

"Worse for the wear?" Shelly finished for him.

"Exactly." He pulled out a chair and sat down as he contemplated how much to tell the women and whether to mention the land sale and the lease. Less was probably more. "The resort is struggling right now. We're trying to turn things around."

"Our movie could put you on the map," Izzy said.

"We'd rather not be on the map looking so neglected."

"Shabby chic," Shelly offered. "It's all the rage."

He winced. "More like just shabby. I know your documentary isn't about the resort, per se, but still, this place will be seen. I'd like to avoid getting publicity that shows us at our worst."

"Everything won't be White Bear Lodge. We're going to shoot at some other resorts, too," Izzy said.

"Are you asking us not to film here?" Shelly took a swallow of her coffee.

He rested his elbows on the table. "No, no. I'm just asking that you be aware of what you're filming. If something looks run-down…consider leaving it out."

"I don't think you have to worry," Shelly said. "No one will mistake our movie for a travelogue."

"We're just taking a nostalgic trip back, that's all," Izzy said. "A glimpse into what things were like back in the day."

Gib gave a reluctant nod of acquiescence. The girls didn't want to pull back on their coverage and he couldn't blame them. After all, they'd already secured his grandfather's permission. That left him only one option—keep an eye on them while they were here and try to gently steer them away from locations that showed the resort in a less-than-desirable light.

Izzy GLANCED AT HER WATCH. "We've got twenty minutes before Pete's coming out. Do you remember the script?"

"Of course. I'm the consummate professional." Shelly fluffed her blond hair and went to stand on the steps leading to the lodge's front door. Behind her, Adirondack chairs lined the veranda like a row of white sails. On the far end, a porch swing rocked gently in the breeze.

Izzy set up the tripod, then framed Shelly in the camera. "Your blouse is gaping."

Shelly pulled the edges of her pale pink blouse together at the bust. "I gain a few pounds and nothing fits anymore."

"Yeah, well, at least you gain it in the right places. The ten I got glued itself onto my hips. You ready?" Without waiting for an answer, she flipped on the camera. "Action." Saying that word out loud sent a thrill through her.

"January 16, 1920, marked the beginning of Prohibition and the start of an era of criminal activity unprecedented in America's history," Shelly said in her television voice. "During the Roaring Twenties and the Heated Thirties, Chicago became known as the crime capital of the world. By 1924, a study by the University of Chicago found that 100,000 gangsters lived—"

"Cut."

"What's wrong?"

"You're talking too fast. Let's try it again. Action."

Shelly pursed her lips in concentration, then spoke again. "January 16, 1920, marked the beginning—"

"Cut."

"What?"

"I forgot to tell you—the first time you left out the thing about the trains."

"Right. Take three." Shelly began again, smoothly adding that as the railroads began luring wealthy Chicagoans to the cool north woods of Wisconsin for vacation, Chicago gangsters joined the summer exodus. "They wanted to escape the heat and be able to relax away from the dangers facing them every day in the city.

For resorts like White Bear Lodge it meant prosperity—"

"Cut."

"It's getting harder by the minute to be the consummate professional."

"Shift to the left a couple of feet. It looks like that hanging plant is sprouting from your head."

As soon as Shelly took the new spot, Izzy said, "Take four. Fix your blouse again. Action."

Shelly slid into her lines, each coming smoothly on the heels of the last. This was going to be so good.

"Ladies, don't tell me I'm late."

Izzy jumped and snapped off the camera. "No. Not at all. We were early so we thought we'd get some of the introductory footage we need."

"What I got on okay to wear?" Pete asked. "I showered again after doing kitchen cleanup."

She took in his baggy khakis and light blue shirt, open at the neck. "Perfect. How are things in the kitchen?"

"Dust from that fire extinguisher is in every nook and cranny. Gonna be a while before we can cook in there again." He gestured at the porch. "So, where you want me?"

"Up on the veranda in front of the chairs. Shelly'll stand off camera and ask you questions. Look straight at the camera and answer the best you can. Don't worry if you make a mistake—just begin again and we'll fix everything in editing."

While Pete was making a practice run, Gib and his grandmother came out the side door to stand beside her. Though the day wasn't extremely hot, suddenly the palms of her hands grew damp. "I think the porch is fine, don't you?" she asked Gib. "Not a bit run-down. And the chairs, well, they'll be in the background. No one will be able to tell they need a fresh coat of paint," she blabbered.

"Thanks." He put a hand on her arm, and the warmth of his touch made her breath catch. "You'll get less glare from the sun if you move this way a little. Plus, then he'll be framed by the porch railing." He held his hands up to form a rectangle, illustrating the shot.

Such a kind gesture, him helping her even though he had reservations about them shooting at the resort. "I see what you mean. Thanks." *Get moving.* They had to keep moving before she swooned. She repositioned the tripod. "Okay, new scene, take one," she called in an overly confident tone. "Why don't we start with an overview of how White Bear Lodge came to be."

Pete cleared his throat a couple of times. "My great-grandfather was a man ahead of his time. He figured folks would someday want to come from the big cities to vacation in the north. So he made a deal with Jeremiah Gordon, the man who owned this land, to give him a hundred-year lease so he could build White Bear Lodge. Before long, Chicago discovered the Wisconsin Northwoods, and as you know, even gangsters want a break from their everyday life."

"Tell us about those days," Shelly said.

Pete rolled into the stories his grandfather had passed on to him, about Prohibition and gambling and shoot-outs. "Though, we never actually had any shoot-outs here," he said. His expression grew thoughtful. "Maybe that's because we have the tunnel to the beach. It actually runs under the house. My grandfather said it was built during Prohibition so they could haul illegal liquor in from a boat on the lake. Seems to me, though, that it would be more useful for escaping if the feds came calling."

Izzy couldn't contain her excited grin. An escape tunnel under White Bear Lodge? She tilted her head around the camera to look directly at Pete. "Can we see it? Film down there?"

Catherine stepped into the viewfinder. "It's closed off at the house end. Years ago, we made a fruit cellar where it comes into the basement. The rest is just dark and dank."

"That's okay," Shelly said. "Even if we can only get into part—"

"It's full of old stuff." Pete shook his head. "We've been using it for storage for a long time."

"Pretty much impassable these days," Catherine said. "Besides, that cluttered mess doesn't need to be seen in a movie." She started for the house, as though the subject was now closed to discussion.

"Neither do the cobwebs, spiders and centipedes," Gib added.

Much as she tried to hold it back, a shudder rippled through Izzy. She had no desire to go into a spider-filled tunnel. Besides, she had more or less promised Gib she would try to show the resort in the best light, and the tunnel definitely sounded like an area of concern. "I'd be fine with filming the entrance at the beach," she said.

"That should be all—" Pete's eyes narrowed as a squad car pulled up in front of the building.

An officer climbed out to saunter toward them. "Hey, folks, hope I'm not interrupting anything."

Shelly stepped forward. "As a matter of fact—"

"Not at all," Izzy said.

"Hey, Butch." Pete started down the veranda stairs.

"What's up? We got the fire under control this morning," Gib said.

Butch held out his hand. "Yeah, I heard about that. You always got something exciting going on out here. Nah, I need to talk to Pete for a couple minutes."

"Take ten, everyone." Izzy sat on the steps and watched the two men move far enough away to have a private conversation, their expressions suddenly serious.

"Gosh, we're laboring so hard, I'm working up an appetite," Shelly muttered facetiously.

"There's a platter of cookies on the dining hall buffet. If you're going in, I'll take one, too." Gib dropped down beside Izzy, his leg brushing against hers. Heat slid through her and she shifted slightly to break the contact.

After a few minutes, the two men shook hands, and Butch drove off.

"What was that about?" Gib asked.

His grandfather shrugged. "Nothing."

"Didn't look like nothing to me. This isn't about any *side business,* is it?"

"Nope. Quit asking so many questions." Pete smiled at Izzy. "Ready for take two, young lady? I don't want to miss my fifteen minutes of fame."

Shelly burst through the door with a fistful of cookies. "I got one for everyone—except you, Pete. We don't want cookies in your teeth on camera." She glanced from one face to the next. "Did I miss anything exciting? What did that cop want?"

"Nothing," Gib muttered, standing.

"Nothing." Pete went back to his mark on the porch and Izzy filed away *side business* to think about later.

IZZY SLUNG THE CAMERA BAG over her shoulder and fell into step beside Shelly as they headed back to their cottage. The sun was high and warm, and dappled the leaves and trail with golden patterns of light.

"That went well," Shelly said. "I think we got some excellent footage."

Izzy nodded absently, her thoughts caught up in the quick conversation Gib and his grandfather had after the cop left. Something was off. "When you were chasing down the cookies in the lodge, Gib asked his grampa if the cop was here about his *side business,*" she said.

"What side business?"

"I don't know. And remember last night? When we were talking to Pete about filming, that guy showed up and wanted to talk about business?"

"Maybe he sells Tupperware or something. Lots of people moonlight." Shelly grabbed a stick off the ground and began to swing it through the brush as they walked.

"Just a feeling I'm getting… I think this family's in a lot of turmoil about the land being sold."

"Well, who wouldn't be?"

Izzy gazed into the branches arching above the trail, green leaves forming a natural canopy. "I can see why they love it here so much. I only wish it wasn't my family selling it out from under them."

"You can't feel responsible for something out of your control. It's your parents' doing—not yours."

Izzy sighed.

"You want me to make you feel better, less guilty? I can do that." Shelly tapped a finger against her lower lip, thinking. "What if...hmm...what if Pete's side business isn't what we think it is?"

"What does that mean?"

"I'm thinking, give me a minute.... What if, aah... Got it! What if his side business is something illegal?"

Izzy snorted.

"I can tell you're feeling better already. Okay, so here's the story. It's totally clear to me now. Pete's involved in...organized crime. In fact, he's been in organized crime all his life. Is your guilt easing now?"

"It would help if the story had a degree of believability."

"It does," Shelly said defensively. "Think about it a minute. Gib wants to restrict where we film here. Why? I'll tell you why. It's not because the resort is run-down. Admit it, this movie would give the place mystique even if it was a complete dump." She swished her stick through the underbrush. "If Gib's goal is really to rejuvenate the business, he should be ecstatic to have us filming here. But is he? No! He's clearly hiding something—"

"That his grandfather is in the Mafia? A man with a nice Irish name like *Murphy?*"

"Exactly. What if ninety years after the Roaring Twenties, gangsters are alive and well in the Northwoods of Wisconsin?" She smacked her stick hard against a tree trunk. "That's what the *side business* is all about." She gave a self-satisfied nod. "*Now* is your guilt about selling the land gone?"

"Oh, yes, completely. I feel so much better knowing that the Murphys are in the Mafia." Izzy began to laugh. "You really outdid yourself this time. I think this was your best ever…concoction."

"I'm just getting warmed up."

"Oh, God, I was afraid you were going to say that."

CHAPTER FIVE

"WHAT DO YOU THINK of those women making the movie?" Gib asked his brother. He leaned against the side of the pinball machine in the game room and watched Matt play, music blasting, lights flashing, bumpers thumping, the steel ball flying over the playing field, and points racking up faster than he could count.

"Hey, get off," Matt said, eyes focused intently on the game. "You're going to make it tilt."

Gib straightened and repeated the question.

"They're okay. Shelly is the better-looking one." Matt punched the right flipper and gave the machine a couple of shakes to make the ball bounce around more.

Was his brother blind? By far, Izzy was the more attractive. "If you're into ditzy blondes. No, I mean, what do you think about them making the movie?"

"Might help business."

"If the resort was in better shape, yeah. But it wouldn't be hard to make this place look bad—"

"Mostly because it does look bad."

"I'd say that nails the issue," Gib said.

Bells jangled as the machine spun through hundreds of extra points.

"What's the big deal?" Matt said. "Be nice to the girls and they'll be nice to you."

"I am nice to the girls."

"Okay, then, what's to worry about?" Matt gently nudged the machine to make the ball bounce around more and up his score. "You should tell Bill Campbell about the movie and how it could help us. Maybe we wouldn't have to do all that other stuff like the brochure and Web site."

"I doubt it. Which reminds me, I've got to find a graphic designer, fast—one who won't charge an arm and a leg."

"At least you won't have to find a photographer."

A chill seeped through Gib. He hadn't picked up a camera since the explosion.

"I mean, you can shoot everything we need, can't you?" Matt jiggled the machine and a buzzer sounded, signaling tilt. He slapped the glass top as he waited for the ball to roll to the bottom.

"We've got millions of pictures around here from all the years we've been in business," Gib said evenly. "There's got to be lots to choose from already."

Matt let out a hoot. "Yeah, maybe we should use some of the ones I shot with Grampa's old Instamatic."

"Maybe."

Hand frozen on the ball launcher, Matt glanced at him. "What? You don't want take the pictures?"

"No, no, I'll do it. No big deal."

His brother launched the last ball into the machine. He played without speaking, the only sound that of the bells ringing and buzzers whirring. "I guess I could take the pictures. I actually did learn some of the things you tried to teach me."

"You trying to cut in on my territory?"

"No. Just thought I could contribute something to the cause."

"How about hard labor? We need to get one of the cottages renovated. Cleaned, repainted. Get rid of those beat-to-shit furnishings. Make the place *cute* so the bank knows we mean business."

"Yeaaah. Cute. That's my specialty." Fingers on the flipper buttons, Matt stayed focused on his game.

The ball spun through the maze, hitting the bottom as the scorer whirred and pinged, adding hundreds of last-second points. Matt grinned at his final score. "Forget cute. I think I'd rather take the pictures."

Gib chuckled to hide the relief he felt at his brother's offer. His camera lay packed away in its case, on a chair in his childhood bedroom. For the first time since he learned how to use a camera, he didn't have an interest in photography.

And he didn't care.

SHELLY PEERED OUT THE COTTAGE kitchen window into the night. "There it is again. A light in the woods," she said in a low voice. "In the dark."

"That's usually where you see lights. In the dark," Izzy said from the living room, not lifting her head from her book.

"Yeah, but what's it doing out there, late like this?"

"Maybe it's fireflies."

"Giant ones? It's a flashlight beam. Maybe it has something to do with that cop coming out to see Pete today. Maybe it has something to do with the *side business*."

Izzy groaned. "In the woods?"

"What if that story I made up was true? Maybe my mind tapped into the energy of this place and I thought I was making it up but it's actually what's really going on."

"Oh. My. God. You've cracked."

"Izzy, try to look beyond your doubts and believe—"

"That the Murphys are into organized crime? Holding secret meetings in the woods?"

"Where else would you hold a secret meeting?"

"Gee, I don't know. In a car? A restaurant?"

Shelly leaned forward until her nose almost touched the window. "Too risky. If you're in the Mafia and want to have a meeting where you can be sure you won't be overheard or the room hasn't been bugged, what would you do?"

"I see your point." Izzy held herself back from laughing. "Clearly, the smart place to go is into a mosquito-infested woods late at night. Hold a meeting by the light of a single flashlight, all the while swatting bugs so you aren't covered in welts the next day."

Shelly sank onto the couch and picked up her *Cosmo* magazine. "Okay, so it doesn't sound practical. That's why it's so brilliant. Who would ever suspect it?"

"It's brilliant, all right."

"Go ahead, make fun of me. I still think I may be on to something." She flipped through the magazine. "Check this out. 'Sexy Moves Your Man Loves That He's Never Told You About.' What I want to know is where are all the articles telling the males of the world the sexy moves women love that we never told them about? How come it's such a one-way pleasure street?

If we ever make any money, maybe we should start a men's magazine like that." She let out a snicker. "Forget the magazine, maybe that's what we should make our documentary about."

"Oh, yeah, that would be interesting. You still want to be the talent?"

"We may have to hire professionals."

"Chicken."

Shelly tossed the magazine onto the couch and flicked off the end-table lamp, sending the cottage into darkness. She sidled over to the window to peer outside again.

"Hey! I'm trying to read." Izzy grinned. "Any spies?"

"There it is, still out there in the same place. If it's someone out for exercise, why aren't they going anywhere?"

With an exasperated sigh, Izzy joined Shelly at the window. "Probably just kids having a beer party or something."

"Out here? No way. Mark my words, something's going on at this resort. A light in the woods that stays in the same place long enough for a clandestine meeting to take place? Fishy, I say."

"Maybe it's aliens."

Shelly gave her a dirty look.

"Okay, okay. You genuinely think the Mafia's back at White Bear Lodge?"

"Maybe they never left," Shelly whispered.

Izzy stared at her, barely able to make out her features in the dull light. "Now I know you're off your rocker. You're serious, aren't you?"

"Think about the side-business meeting and how weird Pete acted afterward. Now lights in the woods?"

"If it's gangsters, I vote for leaving them alone. I don't cherish the thought of getting in a tangle with people who utilize torture and hit men on a regular basis," Izzy said.

"Think of what an interesting angle this could be for our documentary."

"Yeah. Except we'll be buried in the concrete foundation of some building somewhere and we'll never experience the thrill of winning."

"I'm going out there." Shelly reached for her hooded sweatshirt.

"Are you crazy?"

"I'm not going to confront anyone. I'm merely taking a leisurely walk on a balmy summer night." She flipped on the kitchen light and strolled through the living room.

"You are not going. What if…?"

"Nothing's going to happen."

"How do you know? They could have guns…. They could have a spaceship—"

Shelly lifted her chin bravely. "Alien abduction? I'd better take the videocam along, then."

"You're not going out there."

"You're welcome to join me." Shelly slipped the sweatshirt over her head and opened the door.

"Oh, my God. Wait. I'll come just to keep you safe." Izzy pulled on her windbreaker, grabbed a flashlight and followed Shelly outside. "I hope this is some teenagers making out. It would serve you right."

"Shut that light off. We don't want to announce our arrival."

"It's kind of hard to see."

Shelly gestured at the sky. "It's a full moon. The only clouds are thin cirrostratus, which don't block any of the moonlight. Wait a few minutes and your eyes will adjust. Did you bring your cell phone?"

"What for?"

"In case we need to call the police."

"Great. Did you bring yours?"

"Of course. I'm not a total idiot."

Izzy went inside to grab her phone. She couldn't believe she was going along with this. "Okay. I'm ready."

They skirted the edge of the dark woods for a hundred yards, then stepped onto a path heading into the forest. Izzy's stomach began to jump. She could see the steady beam of the flashlight in the distance. After a couple of minutes, she stopped, jittery from adrenaline. "I don't think we should both go all the way there. What if it *is* dangerous—one of us needs to be able to call for help."

"Yeah, if we're both tied to the railroad tracks it might not be so good. You go on ahead," Shelly whispered. "I'll wait here and call the police."

Izzy scowled at her. "No, you go ahead. This was your idea. If it were up to me, I'd be back at the cottage reading my book or working on our script or something." She peered into the woods around them, searching for glowing yellow eyes. "Anything other than waiting to be eaten alive in the woods by mosquitoes…or werewolves."

"Fine. Give me the flashlight." Shelly reached for the light and Izzy held it away from her.

"You're not leaving me alone in the dark without a light. Why didn't you bring one of your own?"

"Izzy. I need to be able to illuminate what's going on."

"And I need to be able to illuminate the path so I can get back to tell the police where you are."

"Nothing is going to happen." Shelly made a grab for the flashlight. "Quit being a baby and give me the light. All you have to do is stand here. If you hear anything odd, dial 911. Your phone is backlit. You can see it in the dark."

Izzy handed over the flashlight and watched Shelly head farther into the woods. A twig snapped behind her and she whirled round, heart pounding. *Breathe,* she told herself. *And focus.* It was probably just a raccoon. Or a possum. Or a *vampire.* Shuddering, she wrapped her arms around her waist and began to softly hum the tune to "My Favorite Things."

Reading. She should be reading right now. Watching television. Going to sleep in a cozy bed. Anything but standing in the woods waiting to be ambushed by…night creatures. She brushed a flyaway hair off her forehead and peered into the blackness toward the mysterious flashlight beam. Then she took her cell phone from her pocket and held it in her hand, ready for an emergency.

Hands down, this had to be one of the dumbest things she'd ever let herself get talked into. She glanced at the illuminated face on her watch. Shelly had been gone for five minutes. A second beam appeared in the darkness close to the first and her heart began to jackhammer. What did it mean? Had Shelly turned on her light? Or were there even more people out there?

Suddenly a shriek shattered the silence. Izzy's heart jumped. Her stomach tightened. The blood began to pound in her ears. A strangled scream followed the first and she dropped to a squat on the ground. She fumbled her phone open and, with shaking fingers, punched in 911. "Help. My friend's in trouble," she whispered. She gulped in mouthfuls of air and quickly described what had happened. "We're at White Bear Lodge. Down a path near Beechwood Cottage. Hurry, because I'm going down there to help and God only knows what I'm going to find."

"Miss, you need to stay put," the female operator said firmly. "We'll have someone there in minutes."

Izzy shut off the phone. She couldn't abandon Shelly. Reaching out a hand, she groped around on the ground until her fingers closed around a sturdy stick. Then she hurried down the path as quietly as possible. As she drew near the glow of the flashlights, she slowed her steps and raised the stick to shoulder level, ready for action. Suddenly Shelly's giggle rippled through the woods toward her, followed by the sound of a familiar male voice. She stopped and squinted into the darkness.

Gib Murphy?

What was he doing out here so late?

Brandishing her stick, Izzy stepped through the underbrush toward Shelly and Gib, furious that she'd had the wits scared out of her. And even more irritated at how utterly cute Gib looked in his sweatshirt, shorts and running shoes. "What's going on?" she demanded. "I thought you were being murdered. I almost had a heart attack." She eyed the shovel in Gib's hand and glared at him. "And what are you doing out here in the dark?"

"Grave digging." He raised both hands in surrender, one still holding the shovel.

Izzy's eyes widened and both Shelly and Gib laughed. "He's only saying that because I told him you thought there were werewolves out here." Shelly shone her light into a plastic ice cream pail on the ground. "That's what he's doing."

Izzy lowered her stick and bent to get a better view. Big fat earthworms writhed around in the black dirt in the container.

"Ugh!" She jerked up and took a quick step back.

"Now you see why I screamed," Shelly said. "He held a shovelful up to me."

"I'm digging night crawlers," Gib said. "Bait. For fishing."

"Out here?"

"They're near the surface because the ground is always damp." He picked up a chunk of freshly over-turned earth and grasped a fat worm between his thumb and forefinger. "Watch. As this guy tries to dig deeper to escape, he'll let go of his grip on the soil—" Gib pulled the night crawler free "—and then he's mine." He dropped the worm into the bucket.

"How fascinating," Izzy said.

"You two ever been fishing?"

"My dad took me a couple times when I was a kid," Shelly said less than enthusiastically.

"No," Izzy said. "Never."

"Never?" Gib straightened. "I'm going out tomor-row. Want to come along?"

"Oh, no, I—"

"You've never been fishing and you're going to say no? Don't you want to do any extracurricular activities while you're here?"

"Actually, extracurricular activities were high on our list," Shelly said.

Izzy cast a sideways glance at her friend. They were?

Gib lifted an eyebrow. "So?"

Worms? On hooks? "Shelly and I have some extensive filming we want to do tomorrow."

"Not anymore," Shelly said. "High pressure is moving in from Canada."

"Which means?" Izzy asked.

"Continued clear skies, lots of sunshine and a nice north-to-northeast wind. Highs around eighty degrees, dry and comfortable air. I could use a little sun time."

"But our documentary—"

"Can wait a couple of hours. If you've never been fishing, you need to try it." Shelly looked at Gib. "Just tell her where and when and she'll be there."

"But—"

"We won't stay out long," Gib said.

"Go," Shelly said. "With my blessing. I really would like some time alone to lie in the sun."

"Come on, Iz," Gib said.

Iz? She huffed. "Fine. What time?"

"Six."

"Six? That's perfect. We'll have all day to shoot the footage we need."

"That would be six a.m.," he said.

Shelly began to chortle.

"In the morning?"

"No use fishing when the fish aren't biting. And they're biting early."

"They know the value of eating a good breakfast." Shelly shone her light into the bucket again and made a face.

"It's amazing that time of the day," Gib said. "The

sun is rising. The air is cool. The birds are stirring, but the rest of the world is quiet. You haven't lived until you've been on a lake in the early morning hours."

Izzy found herself captivated by his enthusiasm. Though she'd have to get up at five-thirty, she suddenly realized that she wanted to experience what he was describing. And she wanted to experience it with him.

"It'll be *beautiful, boy,* you'll love it, I know," Shelly said.

"So, are you in?" he asked.

Before she could answer, blindingly bright lights lit up the woods around them and a man shouted, "Everybody, hands in the air. What the hell's going on out here?"

Izzy threw her arms up to shield her eyes. "Oh, shit."

"What the hell's going on out *there?*" Gib muttered. "Butch?" he yelled. "It's me, Gib. Drop the light down."

As the beam lowered toward the ground, Izzy counted three uniformed police officers and a big German shepherd coming toward them through the woods.

"Gib? I'll be damned. We got a call that one of your resort guests was being attacked."

Shit, shit, shit. Izzy threw an apologetic wince at Gib, then raised a hand and weakly wiggled her fingers. "I think there's been a misunderstanding."

Gib grinned as though this was the best thing that ever could have happened. "6:00 a.m." He sounded like he'd just won the lottery. "And wear a sweatshirt, it'll be cold for a while."

CHAPTER SIX

AT TEN MINUTES TO SIX the next morning, stomach jumping in nervous anticipation, Izzy let herself out of the cottage and headed for the beach. The sun was up over the horizon, its shimmering light signaling the start of another day. It had been a major effort to get out of bed this morning; by the time they'd finished with the police last night it had been past one o'clock.

She inhaled the crisp, pine-scented air. Gib was right—being out early like this made her feel more alive than she had in a long time. Everything was so fresh and still, as though hushed in expectation of another glorious summer day.

Though Shelly had predicted the temperature would reach eighty today, right now it was probably twenty degrees cooler. Izzy zipped up the front of her hooded sweatshirt and swung her beach bag back and forth like a kid. Hopefully they wouldn't be out on the lake so long she'd need anything besides the towel, sunscreen and book she'd brought along.

She paused at the edge of the woods and gasped at the sight of the lake, smooth as glass and bathed in low-lying fog, the pier, the beach, everything, softened as though pale gray watercolor had been brushed over the scene. It was a vision of halves—overhead, the sky brightening with the rising sun, while below was a mystical, silvery world. She watched Gib, barefoot and wearing a navy blue sweatshirt and khaki shorts, toss flotation cushions into a small boat tied to the dock. He bent to secure something in the bottom and his well-defined calf muscles flexed with the movement. She caught her breath for the second time in half a minute. *He is so gorgeous.* Suddenly, Gib looked back and she jerked her eyes higher and waved.

"You're right on time," he called, smiling, eyes warm and welcoming. His dark hair was mussed as though he'd jumped out of bed and headed for the beach without a glance in the mirror. And his clothes were the same ones he'd had on last night, rumpled as though he'd slept in them. Why had she thought him so dangerous that first day? Everything about him was unstructured, appealing in its freeness. So different from Andrew, who not only liked his ducks in a row, but wanted to pick the row they were in and even dictate their every move.

Not that there was anything wrong with that.

As she drew near where Gib waited on the dock, she considered the boat more closely, fifteen feet of dented, blue-painted metal, little more than a rowboat with a motor on the back end, bench seats at the front and rear, and a big flat space in the middle where the center seat had been removed. She hoped it didn't leak. "This is it, huh?"

AT IZZY'S DUBIOUS expression, Gib was torn between putting a reassuring arm around her shoulder and teasing her, but decided against either. She looked adorable this morning, her hair pulled into a ponytail, a pair of sunglasses propped on top of her head. For some reason, he couldn't wait to take her out on the water, show her how much fun fishing could be. "This is it. The blue canoe."

"Canoe?"

"Don't worry, she's plenty seaworthy. That's just what Matt and I used to call it as kids." He gave her a playful pat on the back. "You do know how to swim, don't you?"

"I feel really safe now."

He pointed at a cooler in the bottom of the boat. "I brought us some doughnuts, orange juice and soda."

"And the infamous worms," Izzy said when she noticed the pail next to the cooler.

"That goes without saying."

"But no beer? I thought beer was a staple for fishermen."

"Okay, there's a couple of beers in there, too," he said. "When the fog burns off it can get plenty hot on the lake. Makes you thirsty, all that fresh air and sunshine."

"All that energy expended reeling in those whoppers, I bet."

"That, too. Why don't you climb down onto that front seat. Watch out for the fishing poles on the left." He loosened the lines on the dock.

Izzy stepped into the boat awkwardly and its sudden rocking motion made her lose her balance. She dropped down onto the seat with a thud and let out a nervous giggle.

"Careful." Gib followed her aboard and started the motor. It sputtered a moment, then flared to life. As they pulled away from the dock, Izzy grabbed tight to the gunwale and peeked over her shoulder to ask, "How far are we going?"

He gestured at a string of small islands farther out on the lake. "Great place for catching crappies and blue-gills. Small panfish. Hang on." He gunned the engine and the boat shot forward.

Several minutes later, they were slowly cruising along the shore of the largest island. Gib brought the boat to a stop in the shade beside a big tree that had fallen into the lake, its branches like a labyrinth under the water. "This is a crappie playground." He lowered the anchor into the lake without making a splash and cleated the line. "They love to hang out in brush piles and fallen trees." He rubbed his hands together gleefully. "Let me show you how to bait a hook."

Izzy scrunched up her face. "If it's all the same to you, I think I'll pass on setting the bait today."

He lifted a fat, wiggling night crawler from the bucket and baited her hook, then his. "Next time, then."

"Yeah, next time," she said.

Suddenly it became vitally important to him that she have fun today. He showed her how to cast off. "Keep an eye on your bobber. You'll see it bounce when a fish is nibbling. If you get a bite, it'll pull right down into the water."

After a couple of minutes staring intently at her red-and-white bobber, Izzy shifted in her seat and glanced down at the tackle box. She unzipped her sweatshirt a couple of inches. "How soon, usually, until a fish nibbles?" she asked.

He raised his eyebrows and held back a smile. "Could be a minute. Could be hours. It all depends on how hungry the fish are."

"Oh. Well."

"Don't tell me you're getting bored already," he teased.

"No. But I'm glad I brought a book. Any of those doughnuts custard-filled?"

"Yeah. And they're chocolate-frosted, too."

"Seriously? I'm salivating already."

He felt an irrational delight at having made her happy. Opening the cooler, he dug out two doughnuts—chocolate-frosted for her and powdered sugar for him.

She took a bite and licked custard off her top lip. "You were right about how peaceful it is out here. The lake is so still." She wiggled her fishing pole and watched the movement make her bobber dance, sending tiny ripples over the surface of the water. "It's beautiful."

"But…boring?"

"I'm sure it's an acquired taste." She took another bite of doughnut. "How deep is this lake?"

"In the middle it's probably fifty feet." Gib arranged several cushions against the side and bottom of the boat, then slid down on them, legs outstretched in front of him. "I brought enough cushions so you can get comfortable, too. Makes the waiting easier."

Izzy set up a cushioned corner for herself and leaned back like Gib. "Have you always liked to fish?"

"As a kid, the boredom got to me. Couldn't stand waiting for something to happen. Too young to appreciate the downtime. But I've come out fishing every morning since I got back."

"Back from where?"

He exhaled. He hadn't intended to get on this subject this morning. "Iraq. I was on assignment there."

"That explains your changed opinion about boredom."

"Yeah. There's something to be said for knowing nothing is going to happen."

She tilted her head. "I guess it's all relative. Sometimes I wish something would happen in my life."

"Like what?"

"I don't know. I mean, I know order is important to the universe, but—"

He gave a bitter laugh. "It seems to me the universe thrives on disorder."

She blinked, as though he'd presented an idea she'd never considered before.

"Sorry," he said. "Sometimes I'm too cynical."

She opened her mouth as if she were about to reply, then stopped herself. After a moment, she said, "Do you catch a lot of fish?"

"Some days. Sometimes all I catch is a nap."

"Seems like it would be a good place to get away and think. No interruptions, no noise."

"Mostly I try not to think. I had this dream once when I was in Iraq…that I was sitting out here, taking life easy, not caring whether I caught anything or not. It was incredible to be back and I was wondering why I'd never noticed it before." He rested his head against the boat cushions. *Why the hell was he telling her this?* "I popped open a beer and then, suddenly, a huge sturgeon jumped out of the water into the boat. It thrashed around, creating chaos, and I tried to catch it, but the boat swamped and I ended up in the water, flailing, fighting with the fish and trying not to drown, all the while knowing I was going to lose. And then I woke up. It took me a couple of seconds to realize where I was—about as far away from Menkesoq Lake as I could get."

"You were missing home." She reached across the space between them, rested a hand on his arm for a moment, and he was tempted to pull her beside him just to feel the warmth of another body next to his. He shook his head.

"It was a reaction to the environment I was in. I was missing the safety of home, not home."

"Splitting hairs, aren't you? Missing home. Missing the safety of home."

"No—" He considered the point she was trying to make. "Well, maybe."

Izzy sat up straighter to eye her bobber. "Hey, is that a bite?" She scrambled onto a bench seat and Gib followed her up.

"I think I have a fish!" She bounced on her seat.

"Easy, now. Something's definitely interested. Give him a second to make sure he's hooked."

The bobber pulled beneath the surface, then popped up and was yanked under again.

"Okay, you've got one." He told Izzy what to do, and a few minutes later she'd landed a small bluegill. Holding up the line proudly, the blue-and-yellow fish dangling off the hook, she tossed her head, eyes sparkling with childlike excitement.

"How could I have come out here without my camera?" he asked.

She laughed out loud, the sound light and airy and joy-filled. It was then Gib realized he wanted to put his arms around her not simply to feel the warmth of another person beside him, but to feel the warmth of *her* beside him. "It's a beauty," he said. "But we can't keep it." For a moment he wondered whether he wasn't talking to himself about Izzy. "Too small to keep," he added. He slipped the fish off the hook and tossed it back in the lake, watching as it wriggled on the surface a moment before disappearing beneath the water.

"Going home," Izzy said quietly. "The best place in the world to be when you're hurting."

Gib rebaited the hook, then leaned back into the cushions, wincing a little in pain as he repositioned his left leg. He looked up to see Izzy's eyes on him.

"Can I ask what happened? With your knee, I mean?"

He hesitated only a second before replying. "An explosion. Shrapnel."

"Suicide bomber?" Her eyes narrowed.

"Yeah." *Don't ask me more,* he thought. *I can't go there right now.*

"You came home to recuperate."

"In a sense." *Or to escape.* He didn't know which, didn't really care. "Somehow, though, I've been sucked into trying to turn the resort around. Matt and I are about to update Hickory Hollow—the cottage down the road from yours. Stop by if you see us working."

"Are you doing every cottage?" There was a level of concern in her eyes that he didn't understand.

"Maybe." He sighed. "Remember my grandpa talking about how we lease the land the resort sits on? Well, the owner wants to sell it. According to the lease, the buildings go with the property. If we aren't the buyer, we lose everything."

She nodded thoughtfully. "Are you going to buy?"

"Working on it. We need to get a loan, and the bank…well, let's just say they've got a number of hoops we need to jump through to get approved."

"Like fix up the cottages?"

"That's part of it. Get a Web site…promotional things. Even then, it's pretty iffy." He laced his fingers behind his head. "This place has been in the family so long, none of us can imagine not having Murphys at White Bear Lodge. My grandparents love it here. My brother wants to take over when they retire."

"And you? What about you?"

He dropped his head back and pondered her question as he gazed up at the pale blue sky. "When I was younger, I always wanted out. See the world. Staying put was never my goal. I figured I'd break out in hives if I stayed here too long."

"Wanderlust."

"Yeah."

"Even with your injury you still feel the same?"

He mulled over her question. Did he feel the same? Yeah, he did…didn't he? "I'm only here for the short term, to give them a hand for a while. After a little R and R, it's back to covering the news for me. I like life on the edge. I like not knowing exactly what the next day will bring," he said, though at this moment the words felt hollow.

"Except when you're home."

"Uh, yeah." He smiled at her and when she smiled back, he almost leaned forward and put his mouth on hers. Hell, what was the matter with him this morning?

The silence stretched between them, comfortable and warm like a beach towel left in the sun.

"So, then, um, as far as fishing, this is it? You sit out here and…wait?" Izzy yawned and took a peek at her watch. "Jeez, already past seven."

"That about describes it."

After a minute, she pulled a yellow highlighter and a how-to book on screenwriting out of her beach bag. Gib's bobber began to bounce on the water and he shoved himself up to reel in his line, then lifted the end of the pole to reveal an eight-inch bluegill. "Is this a beauty or what?" He slid the hook from its lip and tossed the fish back in the lake.

"Wasn't it big enough to keep, either?"

Gib baited his hook and cast off again. "If you keep 'em, you have to clean them. I'm big on catch and release."

"Let me get this straight. You've come out here every morning since you got back to *not* catch anything?"

"I catch something," he said defensively.

Her lips slanted up teasingly, and he was struck again by the urge to pull her into his arms and kiss her. "Indeed? What do you catch?"

"Forty winks. It's some of the best sleep I've gotten in months." He slouched into the boat cushions and closed his eyes, thinking that, all in all, it would be a pretty nice day if the only dreams he had were of Izzy in bed beside him.

SHE WATCHED HIM FOR A few minutes, his broad chest gently rising and falling as he drifted to sleep. He'd been something to see reeling in that fish, his hair messy, his jaw dark with a day's growth, his sweatshirt sleeves pulled up above muscled forearms, and his strong hands gently setting the fish free. But there was more to him than just his rugged exterior. Underneath, there was vulnerability and tenderness… And, oh, God, she could almost feel it, there was pain.

She listened to his steady breathing for a few minutes, then yawned and settled into her cushioned corner with her book, shifting from one side to the other in an effort to find a comfortable position. The boat swayed with each move.

"Having some trouble?" Gib murmured.

"I'm sure I'll get this right in a few seconds."

"Lay your cushions here." He rested a hand on the floor next to him. "If we do this right, we can double up the padding."

She hesitated—but only for a second. Carefully moving so she didn't rock the boat too much, she rearranged her cushions and settled in next to Gib. Suddenly ill at ease, every inch of her acutely aware of the man next to her, she opened her book just as he reached around her shoulders and drew her close. Her pulse started to hammer and she forced herself to relax. It was everything she could do to keep from curling into him, putting her head on his chest and going to sleep in his arms to the beat of his heart.

"Isn't this better?" he asked drowsily.

She nodded against his shoulder and tried to read. Within minutes, she was struggling to keep her eyes open; the gentle sway of the boat, the water lapping against the side, the sun raising the temperature even though they were in the shade, all conspired to remind her she hadn't gotten much sleep last night. Finally she gave in to temptation, snuggled closer to Gib and shut her eyes.

"RISE AND SHINE, BEAUTIFUL. Time to head to shore."

She woke to the sound of Gib's voice and struggled to figure out exactly where she was. He'd just called her *beautiful.* She could feel the sun hot against her face, could smell the soft scent of cocoa butter. *Oh, yeah,* she thought lazily, *we went fishing.* She was in the boat. On the lake.

In Gib's arms.

Her eyes flew open. Mortified, she tried to subtly shift away from him, but he wouldn't let her.

"You caught another fish," he said.

She glanced around for her pole. "I did?"

"Uh-huh. Slept right through it. I reeled it in, let it loose, brought both poles into the boat, had some juice and another doughnut. And you didn't even break your snore."

"I was snoring?" Her cheeks began to burn.

"Only a bit."

This was like a bad dream. No doubt she'd been drooling, too. She pulled back in horror. "Really?"

"I'm kidding." His eyes sparkled and he grinned and she thought she would melt from the way he looked right now. *Beautiful Boy.* Shelly was right about that. The sun shimmered in his dark hair and touched his cheeks with gold. She looked at his mouth and swallowed hard, knew she was staring at his lips. And she thought to herself that some women would lean forward this short distance and kiss him. Some women, but not—

And then his mouth was on hers and she wasn't sure which of them had made the move. She closed her eyes and all thoughts fled at the softness of his lips, the taste of orange juice and powdered sugar on his tongue. She trembled at the connection, felt the heat of it race through her, making her dizzy and greedy, and she leaned into him, wanting more. When finally he broke the kiss, she just floated, breathing him in, dazed.

She opened her eyes to find him watching her, his lips curving upward. "Welcome to White Bear Lodge." He tugged his arm from behind her back and pushed himself up onto the bench seat, and she had to hold herself back from begging him to kiss her again.

He started the engine and hauled in the anchor.

Scrambling up onto the front seat, she tried to think of something clever to say. "Does everyone get this special treatment?"

"It's reserved for our favored guests. Unfortunately, any follow-up favored guest activities will have to be scheduled for later because I have to go to work."

Izzy glanced at her watch in disbelief. "I slept three hours?"

"Easy to do out here." He put the engine into forward gear and headed the boat for home.

Ten minutes later, they were back at the dock. Though it was still morning, the beach was already busy with children swimming and adults stretched out in lounge chairs, reading. Izzy helped Gib hang the boat cushions inside the boathouse, then thanked him for taking her.

"Come along anytime." Cooler in one hand, he stepped toward her. "I'd love to have you." Then he bent and kissed her again and her stomach trembled as her face grew hot.

"O-okay. I'll think about it." She held in a giddy laugh as she backed out the door and hurried toward the path to her cottage.

"HEARD YOU WENT FISHING this morning," Matt said with a smirk.

Gib unpacked Hawaiian leis, grass skirts and tiki

torches from a box he'd pulled from the storage room and laid them out on one of the tables in the dining hall. "So?" He tried to ignore the memory of how Izzy had curled into him and fallen asleep, how warm and soft she'd felt in his arms.

"Making friends." Matt grinned and hung a lei around his neck. "Tonight I think I'll make *friends* with Shelly."

"She's probably got ten years on you," Gib said.

"Hey, I'm just doing my part to make sure the resort is shown at its best in the movie."

His grandmother entered the dining hall carrying a laundry basket. "Do you think this Hawaiian luau will help?"

"It's not a luau, it's a beach party," Gib said.

"At least it'll help put the grease fire out of everyone's minds." Matt tied a bright green grass skirt around his waist and began to hula around the room.

"Yeah, and if the beach party doesn't, watching you sure will," Gib said.

His grandmother dropped the basket on the floor and lowered herself into one of the old wooden dining chairs. "But don't luaus have special food like poi and pork—"

"That's why we're not having a luau. We're having a beach party. Wear your floral print shirt and flip-flops…"

"Couldn't we make burgers on the grill again like last night? I don't think anyone cared that the kitchen was out of commission." She looked tired as she began to fold the clean towels.

"As long as we can't use the kitchen yet, we might as well make the meal memorable. Most of the guests never got the hot breakfast they ordered yesterday.

And with the kitchen still down, they didn't get one this morning, either." He pictured Izzy eating her doughnut on the boat, licking chocolate frosting off her upper lip, her cheeks flushing pink when he kissed her....

He pressed his hands flat against the table and leaned his weight forward as he took a slow breath. He should never have kissed her. She was a guest at the resort. She was staying only a week or two. And she was filming a movie that could, in some respects, help make or break White Bear Lodge. Getting involved with Izzy could screw everything up. He forced his thoughts to the issue at hand. "We need to overcome the black marks we got with our guests yesterday. That's why it has to be shish kebab tonight."

"If you say so."

"Grandma, I know the fire and cleanup did you in. You've been working too hard. So if you run a couple of errands into town for us, Matt and I will take care of everything else."

She sighed. "You're sure this will help?"

"If I were a betting man, I'd put my money on it."

"How much?" his grandfather asked with a grin as he appeared in the kitchen doorway. "I'll take that wager."

Gib rolled his eyes. "*That* is exactly why we're doing this. So you never have to take up that damn side business again."

CHAPTER SEVEN

"I THINK YOU HAVE A SERIOUS admirer." Shelly picked up a tube of aloe vera lotion from the drugstore shelf. "'Soothing for sunburns,'" she read aloud.

"What?"

"'Soothing for sunburns.'"

"Not that. The serious thing."

"Don't be coy," Shelly said. "Beautiful Boy. Gib Murphy. From the first minute he brought up fishing, it was obvious he wanted to take you along."

Izzy's heart began to beat a staccato rhythm. She bent to peruse the ingredients in a bottle of green herbal sunburn spray. "Your imagination is running wild again."

"He kissed you. And then he walked you back to the cottage after fishing, for God's sake."

"I walked myself home."

"Okay, but he kissed you."

"Twice." Izzy felt a rush as she remembered. "But it's nothing serious—just a cruise ship romance sort of thing."

"Ack, you have a dreamy look on your face, like a cartoon character in love. I'm not complaining, mind you. He's a heck of an improvement over Andrew."

"What do you have against Andrew?"

"Nothing, as long as you're okay with spending the rest of your life as a Stepford wife."

"He's not that bad," Izzy said, though she had to admit sometimes he was. She took the lotion from Shelly and lifted the bottle of sunburn spray off the shelf. "Come on, lobster girl, let's go. I can't believe you let yourself get so burned."

"I didn't let myself do anything. If you had woken me up when you got back from all those hours of *fishing,* I wouldn't have lain out in the sun so long."

"I was back by ten-thirty—"

"But I didn't wake up for another hour."

"How could I know you took to the chaise at eight?"

Outside the store, Shelly began to rub the cooling lotion into her red arms. "Not only did you not wake me up," she continued, "but you're out fishing for four hours, bring home none, report two kisses, and that's it? No other stories to tell? Highly suspicious."

"I told you—nothing happened. That was the problem. It's definitely a sport for patient types. We got a couple of nibbles and then nothing the rest of the morning."

"Nibbles in the boat and kisses in the boathouse. He sounds smitten."

Izzy held up a stop-sign hand. "You're crazy. It happened because of the mood, the moment—he's not interested in me." A warmth spread through her chest and into her belly. The morning had been wonderful, not a care in the world except whether the fish were biting— and hoping they weren't. It had felt so comfortable talking to Gib, so natural to sleep with his arms around her—

"Hey, isn't that Grandma Murphy?"

Izzy turned to see the diminutive gray-haired woman give a small white envelope to a man in the parking lot across the street. He tucked the envelope in the breast pocket of his suit coat and grasped her hand before getting into a silver Lexus and driving away.

"Oh, ho, what's going on over there? Payoffs?"

Izzy groaned. "It might help to remember that your secret meeting in the woods last night was a night crawler dig."

"Catherine," Shelly called. She headed into the street with Izzy tagging behind, muttering, "You are certifiably insane."

Catherine spotted them and smiled. "Hello, girls. Are you coming to the beach party tonight?"

"What beach party?" Shelly squeezed some aloe vera lotion into the palm of her hand and rubbed it into her burned forehead.

Catherine clucked her tongue. "Gib said he would stop by your cottage to let you know."

Shelly laid a fabulous white-toothed smile on Izzy. "He did?" she asked in a pleased voice. "That's sure nice of him. But here we are in town, getting sunburn lotion."

"We've been gone awhile." Izzy glared at her friend. "Shelly burnt herself but good this morning."

"Might want to rub yourself down with some vinegar. Takes the pain away and turns it to tan."

"White vinegar or cider?" Shelly asked.

"Either will do, I guess," Catherine said. "Stop up at the lodge when you get back. I've got a big jug in the pantry." She began to search through her purse. "I need to pick up a few things… The boys are decorating the beach. We'll be having shish kebabs and strawberry daiquiris—Matt made a list of things to pick up for that. I was just going into the grocery."

"Do we dress in theme?" Izzy asked.

"Anything beachy is what the boys are talking about. Starts at five-thirty. Now, if I can only find that list… I suppose I could call home…" Suddenly she stuck a hand in the pocket of her yellow slacks and triumphantly pulled out a torn piece of envelope. "Thank goodness, there it is!" She headed through the automatic door into the grocery store.

"See you tonight," Shelly called after her.

As soon as the door swung shut, Shelly hooked her arm through Izzy's and began to tug her down the street. "Did you see the back of her shopping list?"

"No."

"It read, *Saints 24.* What do you suppose that means?"

"She's in a Bible study?"

Shelly wrinkled her nose.

"Did you sunburn your brain today, too? Don't even waste one second telling me you think something's going on here. It was a piece of an envelope that someone scratched a note on. *That's it.*" Izzy opened the car door and got inside while Shelly jumped into the passenger seat.

They looked at each other for a long moment. Finally Shelly dropped her head. "I don't know what's wrong with me. Nothing illegal is going on here." She leaned back in her seat and grinned mischievously. "But, what if—"

"Stop! You've succeeded! If you say one more word

about illegal activity or Mafia the rest of the time we're here, I will drive straight to the airport and leave you behind to walk."

BY DINNERTIME, GIB WAS THINKING there had to be an easier way to make the resort successful. No wonder his grandparents were looking so tired. He and Matt had worked feverishly to get everything ready on time. He'd cut up big bowls of peppers, onion, tomatoes and marinated steak, while Matt had gone all out on the fruit salad, cutting several scooped-out watermelons into basket shapes complete with handles, then filling them with melon, cantaloupe, grapes, strawberries and blueberries.

Now, with the torches up and lit, the party was underway. The sun was low on the horizon, casting its golden glow on the beach, Jimmy Buffett was singing about paradise from the portable CD player on a nearby picnic table, and a balmy, light wind rustled the leaves. If you squinted, you could almost believe you were at an island paradise, Gib thought as he handed out grass skirts to the arriving guests.

"What the hell, Matt?" He nodded at the melon baskets. "You've really gotten in touch with your feminine side."

"It takes a real man to know when to be a woman." Matt surveyed the party, now nearly thirty strong. "This is everyone, isn't it?"

"Except our resident moviemakers."

"They're here. Over by the grill."

Gib spotted Izzy and couldn't drag his eyes off her. Izzy, in a floral-print sundress, her hair straight and shiny, her nose and cheeks pale pink from their morning on the water. The phrase *California girl* came to mind even though she was from—where was she from? "Ladies, welcome to Daiquiri Beach. Where the sun is hot, the drinks are cold and your every whim is our command."

"Every?" Shelly asked.

"Within reason," he answered smoothly. "Would you like to start with a strawberry daiquiri?" He picked up a clear pitcher filled with the icy red beverage.

"And how about a lei?" Matt held up the colorful floral necklaces. "I'm in charge of leis tonight."

"Matt," he warned.

His brother grinned. "They don't mind."

"They just humor you." Gib handed each woman an acrylic glass, then took a swallow of his own. "Aah, the sweet taste of a tropical getaway. Enjoy."

The party kicked into full gear with much eating, drinking, laughing and dancing. By the time the sun had gone down in a blaze of orange and pink, most of the guests had returned to their cabins and the number of people present had dwindled to exactly four—Gib, Matt, Izzy and Shelly—sitting at a picnic table at the water's edge, enjoying the night and drinking daiquiris. The heat of the day lingered in the air and the sand. The Beach Boys played on the CD player. And Shelly, wearing one of the grass skirts over her plaid bermuda shorts, got up and began to dance her way down the dock. "This is what summer is supposed to be like," she said lazily. "Hot nights, hot…" She beamed sloppily at Gib. "Hot friends. Don't you think, Busy Izzy?"

Izzy turned to Gib. "She's getting a little *happy*."

"But fun happy," Matt said.

"Hot nights. Hot friends. Cold lake," Shelly yelled. She ripped off the grass skirt, then leaped off the end of the pier, squealing as she hit the cool water. Moments later she burst to the surface and splashed her way to shore, climbing onto the dock again. "Come on in, you guys. The water's fine! Feels wonderful on a sunburn." She jumped into the lake again and peppered them with droplets.

"Somehow, I don't see a lot of filming taking place tomorrow," Izzy said.

Gib got the impression it didn't bother her all that much.

Shaking the spray off his arms, Matt set down his glass.

"Oh, no. I should have known." Gib groaned.

Matt pulled off his Hawaiian shirt, kicked off his sandals and darted down the dock. "Hey! Top this!"

"Run!" Gib pushed himself to standing, grabbed Izzy's hand and raced in the opposite direction.

Matt leaped into the air and hit the water like a cannonball, sending spray flying in every direction.

Wayward sprinkles hit Gib's back as he and Izzy beat their retreat. "Did he get you?" he asked.

"Not too much."

Still holding hands, they watched the two cavorting in the water like kids. Gib felt a quick wave of pure happiness, something he hadn't experienced in months. Maybe even years.

"I'll rescue our drinks," Izzy said. "Before they're full of lake water."

She let go of his hand. The warm night air caressed

his palm and he felt a pang of missing her. Glancing her way, he took in the softness of her countenance, her brown hair blowing loosely around her face in the gentle breeze. She'd invaded his thoughts more than once since they'd gotten back from fishing this morning. And he'd forced her out of his mind each time. He knew better than to let anything more happen between them.

From the water's edge, Matt spotted Izzy heading for the picnic table. "Enemy invaders!" he shouted, sprinting back onto the dock.

At his shout, Izzy seized a glass in each hand and was scampering back toward Gib just as Matt hit the water again. Huge droplets rained down on her and she let out a screech, joy lighting up her face, eyes glistening in the firelight. Every thought about not getting involved dissolved beneath his attraction to her, and he reached out his arms and gathered her in as though it were the most natural thing in the world.

And then he kissed her. A small kiss, impulsive, a brush on the lips, the kind of kiss that seems to come from out of nowhere, driven by the moment. As he pulled away, her eyes met his, her expression full of warmth…and questions.

"Hey, what are you two doing?" Matt hollered.

"None of your business," Gib shouted back. What was he doing? He looked at Izzy. "We…shouldn't be doing this," he said.

She took a step back. "Didn't even happen."

Shelly and Matt traipsed toward them, dripping wet and still screwing around.

"We're going to dry off and change clothes. Then we're taking the golf cart to the Stop on Inn." Matt poured the last of the daiquiri into his and Shelly's glasses. "You two up for it?"

"Not me," Gib said quickly before his mouth had a chance to say something else.

"Me, neither."

Matt shrugged and handed Shelly her glass. "Gonna miss all the fun. Come on, Shellfish."

"See you later, you two." Shelly waved at them.

"Shellfish?" Izzy said. "Now, that's a first."

Gib shook his head. Matt might be taking the *entertain the guests* thing to a new level, but, if Shelly was willing, well, then who was he to complain?

"I'm pretty wet." Izzy finished her daiquiri. "Maybe I should call it a night."

Gib stuck his hands in his pockets, wanting to touch her and knowing he shouldn't. It was good they'd agreed to pretend the kisses had never happened. That way they could go on with life as usual.

Yeah, right. As long as he could ignore the feelings building inside him.

IZZY'S CELL PHONE RANG during the night, awakening her from a sound daiquiri-enhanced sleep. "Hello?" she answered groggily, dragging herself out of a dream. Gib had come up behind her on the pier and kissed the back of her neck and she'd turned and wrapped her arms around him and he'd pulled her tight to him as his mouth found hers—

"Hi, sweetheart," Andrew said.

Her stomach took a panicked leap and the dream dissipated. "Is something wrong? No one's hurt, are they?"

"No. Everyone's fine."

She glanced at the nightstand clock. It was a quarter past midnight. The dream slid forward into her consciousness again, Gib kissing her, the heat between them. She drew in a slow breath to steady her pulse—not sure whether it was racing because she'd been jarred awake by the phone or because she was remembering Gib's kiss. "You almost gave me a heart attack, calling in the middle of the night."

Gib's mouth closed over hers and she forced the memory away.

"Sorry. I left a message earlier, and when you didn't call me back, I got worried."

"We were at a cookout at the beach." She sat up and propped a couple of pillows behind her back. "What do you need?"

"It can wait."

"Andrew, I'm wide awake. What is it?"

"I wanted to see if you've given any thought to what we discussed."

"You mean the night before last?" She flicked on the reading lamp beside the bed and went down the hall, peeking into Shelly's room and noting that her friend was still out on the town with Matt. "Andrew, I understand all your points, but I want to make this documentary. I don't think my making a movie is going to derail our future."

"Sure it could, if you decide to change careers."

Izzy's head felt like it might explode. For a long time, she had liked Andrew's need for control. It made life easy. She never had to worry about a thing because Andrew had the details organized. What movie to watch? Which play to attend? He'd read all the reviews, knew which were getting two thumbs up. What restaurant for dinner? Same thing; he always knew. What color should she paint her living room? Andrew was even up on the latest trends in decorating. She sat on the sofa. He liked being in control and, well, she'd liked him being there.

Until now.

"Izzy? You there?"

Somehow, the arrival of that letter she'd written herself in high school had changed everything for her. And now she couldn't imagine a lifetime in this relationship. "I need to ask you something," she said quietly. "When you asked me to marry you, did you listen to my reply?"

"Of course. I always listen."

Her shoulders slumped. He always listened. But he only heard what he wanted to hear. "I said I would think about it."

"I know."

"Andrew…" she said evenly. "That wasn't a yes."

"Well, right," he said, having the decency to at least sound sheepish. "I probably shouldn't have jumped to conclusions, but we've been dating a year, and I do know you. And it felt like you were putting off saying yes just because you were making this documentary and that maybe you needed me to make the decision."

"For me?"

"For both of us."

Izzy swallowed hard. *The perfect man.* How had she ever thought him that? "Andrew, I feel like we're two people sitting in a boat and rowing in opposite directions."

"If you just turn around we don't have to be."

Her face flushed with heat. Would he never get it? "See, that's the thing. What we each want right now is completely different—"

"I don't think we're that far apart."

"Trust me, we are," she snapped. Instantly regretting her tone, she pulled back. "I think what we need is a break."

"Izzy, now, don't overreact."

"I'm not."

"Don't be afraid to say you need a couple more days to—"

"I don't! I need a break! No, not a break—"

"That's my girl."

Not a break. A breakup, she wanted to scream, but she couldn't bring herself to be that harsh. She sighed. "Andrew, I don't need a couple of days. I need a break. Time off from us."

"Izzy—"

"And it's late. I have a lot of work to do tomorrow. I have to go." Shaking, she closed her phone and let her head drop back, only then realizing she had hung up on Andrew twice in as many days. Only this time, she had ended their relationship.

And she couldn't feel anything but relief.

Then relief was gone, replaced by disappointment with Andrew for the way he was, with herself for putting up with him, with everyone who thought he was so perfect—

What would people think about this?

She clasped her hands together tightly, feeling a lightness fill her as she realized she didn't care how people reacted to this development. That was her mother's way of thinking—not hers.

She was free. Tonight she'd regained her life and, now, the world was hers for the taking.

Fifteen minutes later, wired beyond belief, she marched up the road toward the main lodge intent on finding something to make her sleepy—a glass of milk, turkey, even another daiquiri if need be. The temperature had dropped again—great sleeping weather if you could sleep—and she was glad she'd grabbed a sweatshirt on her way out the door.

Everything was quiet at the lodge, one small light shining in the main entrance, the spacious stone building cozy and welcoming with its bentwood tables and Northwoods decor. In the hearth, a fire still smoldered.

She cut through the dimly lit dining room and got herself a mug of milk from the kitchen, then headed for the sofa facing the hearth. In the shadowy darkness, she spotted someone slouched down into one end of the couch, feet up on the round wooden coffee table. Gib. Sound asleep.

She froze, watching him, reliving the kisses they'd shared. His hands had felt so good on her, she wished— *Stop it.* She reminded herself that they'd agreed to forget anything had happened between them. Gib was dealing with so many issues and she was following her dreams and, really, it was the only logical thing to do.

She set her glass on the table and knelt to stoke the fire, then sat back on the floor, arms resting on her knees as she watched the flames flare and lap at the logs. The dancing red-and-yellow blaze was mesmerizing, relaxing, and she felt her anger toward Andrew begin to ease. She was as much at fault as he for the way their relationship had been.

She sipped her milk, enjoying being on the floor close to the fire, the heat wrapping around her like a cocoon.

"What are you doing here this time of night?" Gib's low, sleep-laden voice startled her from her reverie. He shifted to a more upright position.

"Couldn't sleep. I thought some milk might help." She lifted her glass as if to prove her words. "What's your excuse?"

"Couldn't sleep, either."

"Looks like you were doing okay right now."

"Yeah. I do all right when I reach exhaustion."

She cocked her head, remembering his comments about taking a nap every day when he was fishing. "As long as you're not in a bed?"

He shrugged. "Sleep's funny. It's the only time when your guard is fully down. Problem is, then the stuff you don't want to remember decides to muscle its way in."

What memories was he running from? The explosion that caused his injury? "So you try to fool yourself into thinking you're not going to bed, then doze off whenever, wherever, it hits?"

"That's about it."

Izzy's throat tightened. She wished she knew something to say that would help him. Six years as the traffic coordinator for a cable TV station didn't exactly give her a background in psychology. "Have you tried taking sleep aids?"

"Yeah. The stuff strong enough to work makes me groggy the next day. Only get five hours out of it, anyway. Not worth the trouble."

"So you fish."

A slow smiled lightened his face. "So I fish."

"You want some milk? They say it helps. I could get you some." What she really wanted to do was put her arms around him, help him get past the pain that was keeping him up at night.

"Tryptophan. Supposed to make you sleepy."

"That's right." She went into the kitchen and returned a couple of minutes later to hand him a full glass. "I even heated yours up so you get the added benefit."

"Yum, nothing like warm milk. Thanks." He took a drink.

She lowered herself onto the other end of the couch and stared at the fire, all the while trying not to think about kissing him and wondering if he was having any of the same thoughts. She cast a sideways glance his way and discovered he'd drifted back to sleep, the half-finished glass of milk on the table in front of him.

She yawned and eyed the mantel clock, its hands showing one o'clock had passed ten minutes ago. Time for her to sleep, as well. She gazed at Gib, grateful for his sake that at least he'd been able to conquer his demons for a few minutes more.

Standing, she took the woven throw from the back of the sofa and tucked it over him. His hand closed on her forearm and his other came up to caress the curve of her neck. Eyes open to seductive slits, he drew her head gently downward until her mouth was almost touching his. "Izzy. Thank you…" he murmured sleepily. Then he kissed her, his lips pressing warm and soft, the tip of his tongue brushing against her mouth and dipping inside. The hand at her nape slid up into her hair as he slanted his mouth across hers. And then as quickly as the kiss began, it ended. His eyes locked with hers for a moment, appraising, the desire in them so apparent she almost shivered. "Stay with me," he whispered. "Just to sleep. Here on the couch."

She hesitated in confusion and indecision. Less than an hour ago she'd ended her relationship with Andrew, and already she was kissing another man. She took a step back and he let go of her arm. "Sorry," he said flatly.

"Good night, Gib." She pulled the blanket higher on his chest. "Sweet dreams."

She hurried for the door, wishing she had the nerve to stay with him, wanting nothing more right now than to fall asleep on the couch with his arms around her. And terrified of what it would mean if he ever found out her family was selling the land out from under him.

HE WAS AT THE CAFÉ, a corner bistro in France that sold the best croissants and espresso he'd ever had in his life. It was spring, the air was fresh and he was a freelance photographer again, worrying about money and how to make enough of it to survive. He knew, somehow, that this wasn't real, people don't go back in time, but when Terry came through the door, he buried the knowledge that he was dreaming and waved a hand at his friend, overjoyed to see him again.

This was where they'd met the first time. Terry was fifteen years older and way wiser. The man who'd gotten Gib an in with the Associated Press. Three other journalists joined them, and the discussion turned to the stories they were chasing down, the interviews they needed to get. Alex flirted with the waitress like he always did. Chris was talking about the book he wanted to write.

Thunder cracked, the air darkened and the others went to see what was happening outside. Gib tried to warn them to stay in the café, but he couldn't form the words. He pushed out of his chair and sprinted forward, reaching the doorway as a white bolt of lightning shot earthward. When it passed, only Terry was left in the street, a gray figure almost lost in the downpour. Gib lunged toward him, grabbed his arm, felt the warmth of his skin as the lightning flashed again. He threw an arm up to shield his eyes from the blinding light and dragged his friend backward into the café. The door swung shut behind them, and he opened his eyes to find he held a branch and nothing more. His friend was gone, and outside, the torrential rain pounded the ground in the darkness.

He woke, overcome with grief. Terry had died. The big man with the big heart, and a wife and two little girls at home. The man to whom he owed his success, the man who'd taken him under his wing and taught him how to be a photographer when he was a naive twenty-one-year-old chasing adventure. Terry was gone. And even in his dreams, Gib couldn't save him. He let an arm fall across his forehead and wept.

CHAPTER EIGHT

EARLY THE NEXT MORNING, Izzy and Shelly cut across the dewy grass on their way to the beach intent on figuring out which camera angles to use when they filmed the escape tunnel. Though Pete hadn't brought it up again, Izzy planned to, as soon as she found a way to make a door look interesting.

"Okay, spill all." Shelly sipped the coffee she'd brought along in a travel mug. "What was that kissing thing going on with B.B. last night?"

"What kissing thing?"

"You are such a bad actor. Come on. Tell."

Izzy shrugged, not wanting to let on about seeing Gib later that night. "Who knows? He just kissed me."

Shelly began to chortle. "You mean out of the blue he locked lips? No words? No eye contact? Nothing? Just…smack?"

"Basically."

"I so knew he was interested. Didn't I tell you that from the first day?"

"You're beginning to sound like a broken record."

"Didn't I?"

"What happened with you and Matt last night?" Izzy asked, hoping to change the subject. She raised her sunglasses to peer at her friend.

"No biggie. We went to that bar down the road. This thing with you and Gib is way more interesting. So, when did you get home?" She stopped walking to take a drink of her coffee.

Izzy shook her head. "Don't get too excited. I left the beach right after you did. Andrew called last night…."

"Super," Shelly said flatly.

"We had a fight."

"De duper! So what'd you fight about?"

"Making the documentary." She sighed at the memory.

"Again? Is he going to call about this every day?"

"Not anymore."

Shelly frowned. "What's that supposed to mean?"

In the light of day, Izzy almost couldn't believe she'd had the strength to do the unthinkable last night. "I told him we needed to take a break. We're through."

Shelly made a strangling sound and raised her arms to the morning sky. "Oh, great weather gods, we're making progress down here." She regarded Izzy thoughtfully. "And how do you feel about this?"

A vision of Gib on the couch asking her to spend the night with him popped into her head, and with it came all of her yearning. "I feel mah-velous."

"I can relate. I just won fifty bucks." Shelly stuck out a hand. "Pay up, baby."

Izzy huffed. "Later. We have work to do." She pointed at the small wooden boathouse built into the hillside sloping down to the lake. "There it is. Who would have guessed it's actually the exit from an escape tunnel?" She perused the empty beach. "When we shoot this, let's do it in black and white at dusk. Simulate an escape. Someone running to a powerboat at the dock and—"

"Someone? There's you and there's me."

"Maybe Gib would do it."

"You think you might have an in with Beautiful Boy?" Shelly teased.

"Stop it. Maybe Matt would do it, too. The shot would be a lot more interesting with people. Otherwise it's nothing more than a boring, dare I say it, run-down, building." She propped open the boathouse door so daylight could filter into the room. "I mean, what's exciting about this view? You can't even see a doorway."

Shelly began to dig through the life jackets and other equipment hanging on pegs. "This wall backs up to the hillside. It's got to be right here somewhere."

"Obviously well hidden." Izzy lifted a couple of oars off U-hooks and set them in the corner.

"Look—here are the hinges." Shelly ran her fingers along a well-disguised door edge, flush with the wall. "But no handle."

"Just a wild guess, but maybe it's because they want people to keep out." Izzy stood back.

"Nah." Shelly grabbed a small metal gardening shovel from one of the shelves, stuck the tip into the crack between the door and wall and pressed hard for leverage.

"Pete did say he'd show it to us," Izzy said with a smile.

The door creaked and shifted a little. "Did you see that?"

Izzy bent forward.

The door popped out a crack and Shelly grasped it with her fingers, forcing it open a foot. Cool, musty air slipped out from the dark space. "We're in!"

"Shelly, I don't think—"

"That's right, don't think. Let's go get a flashlight so we can see inside." She pushed the door shut, then grabbed Izzy by the arm and took off for the cottage.

Ten minutes later, they were back, flashlight in hand. At the sight of an elderly couple settling into lounge chairs in the sun, they stopped on the trail. Shelly groaned. "The Steinmetzes. They spend every spare minute on the beach."

"Guess the tunnel's out."

"No way. You distract them and I'll sneak into the boathouse to get the door open. Then you come in—"

"Don't you think they'll wonder why I'm not coming *out* of the boathouse?"

"Tell them you're going to organize the life jackets or something." Shelly took the flashlight and set off, motioning behind her back at Izzy to get moving.

How did she let herself get talked into this stuff? Izzy positioned herself so the couple had to turn away from the boathouse to talk to her. "Good morning," she chirped. "Another beautiful day, isn't it?" She chattered on about the weather until she saw Shelly slip into the boathouse. "I guess I should quit procrastinating. I told the Murphys I would organize the life jackets so…I'm off. If you hear any banging around in there, that'll be me working."

She practically skipped to the boathouse. Inside, she saw the tunnel door wide open and a light flickering in the darkness. Her stomach took a nervous leap. "Shelly?" she whispered.

The light began to move toward her and Shelly appeared, grinning. "It's definitely a tunnel. Come on."

"I'm not going in there. You heard Catherine—"

"There's nothing stored at this end. We'll take a quick peek around and get out. What if there's something in here that would make your movie even better? Old machine guns or bootleg whiskey jars."

Izzy hesitated, then gave in as curiosity got the better of her. "Let's test it first, to make sure we don't get stuck in there." She closed the door on Shelly and seconds later, her friend shoved the door open.

"It doesn't lock. Let's hurry up before any more people come to the beach." Shelly gave Izzy a push, then stepped into the tunnel and pulled the door shut behind them.

"I'll hold the flashlight." Izzy took the light and ran the beam over the tunnel's cement walls and floor, across the stringy cobwebs dangling from the ceiling. A shiver ripped through her in the cool dampness. "I hope there aren't tons of spiders in here."

"Or rats."

"Thanks for that." She aimed the beam ahead, nervously shining it on the walls and ceiling. A spider nearby scrambled away from the light and she jumped, letting out an abbreviated scream.

"Shush!"

"Doesn't seem like anyone's been in here in a long time," Izzy whispered.

"Or else they don't vacuum. Maybe they want it to look this way so no one suspects they're still using it."

"They are still using it—to store junk." She narrowed her eyes as she regarded her friend. "I wasn't kidding before—not another word about the Murphys and organized crime or I'm out of here."

As they stepped deeper into the tunnel they came

upon all the things that been stored away in the decades since the lodge was built—stored away and probably forgotten. Old dressers and headboards, broken wicker lawn chairs, a cane fishing pole, a couple of big gray pickle crocks, and wooden crates filled with yellowed books and magazines—*Liberty, McCall's* and *Life.* "Check out this old newspaper," Izzy whispered. "It's dated 1933. Chicago Bears Win First National Football League Title. Bet this is a collector's item."

"All this stuff is. But it's sure not as cluttered in here as Catherine made it sound."

A minute later, they came to a door at the end of the tunnel. "I thought they said it was closed off," Izzy said. She shone the flashlight on the door, then let the beam slide along several old apple crates stacked against the tunnel wall.

"Apparently not." Shelly turned the knob and tugged open the door to reveal a narrow room, clearly the family's fruit cellar. Jars of jam, fruit and vegetables lined some of the shelves. Others were stacked with early twentieth-century soda cracker tins, cream-colored enamel pans, old shoe boxes, empty mason jars and ceramic vinegar jugs.

"They could make a fortune at an antique store," Izzy whispered. She stepped into the room and picked up a brown Gettelman beer bottle. "Wonder who drank this?"

"Probably Al Capone." Shelly ran a finger down a dusty kerosene lantern. "This stuff would be perfect to set the scene in the documentary," she said in a hushed voice. "It's circa 1920 for sure."

"Yeah, but how can we know about it? We're not

even supposed to be in here." Izzy lifted an old cigar box from one of the top shelves. "Maybe some gangster smoked these on his vacation." She flipped open the lid and discovered the box contained old handwritten receipts. Frowning, she put the box back on the shelf, feeling suddenly like she was nosing around in someone else's personal business. "Let's get out of here," she whispered.

"Just a second. Shoot that light down here." Shelly pulled an old wooden apple crate filled with black ledger books from the bottom shelf.

Izzy held the light high and peered over her friend's shoulder as Shelly opened the top book and riffled through the pages. Each yellowed sheet was similar to the last, with rows and columns of first names, dollar amounts and dates, all written in neat cursive, the blue ink faded with age.

"Check this," Shelly said. "It's from 1991. Miami Dolphins, New York Jets, San Francisco 49ers—this lists every professional football team and the scores of their games at each quarter."

Juggling the flashlight, Izzy picked up a ledger labeled 1993 to find more of the same. She ran a finger down a column. "November 14. Cowboys 20, Cardinals 15. Packers 19, Saints 17." *Saints?* "*Saints?* Ohmigod, Shelly, the envelope that Catherine had—"

"It wasn't a Bible study."

"Let's get out of here."

Shelly slid the wooden box back onto the shelf and the two slipped into the tunnel, quietly closing the door behind them.

"I was joking, you know, about gangsters. I didn't

actually think there was something going on here." Shelly stopped to stare at the crates they had hurried past in their eagerness to see what was on the other side of the door. "More of the same," she whispered. "Ledgers."

Izzy illuminated the boxes as her friend opened the top couple of record books. "These are old ones, too," Shelly said.

"So, whatever they were doing, they quit long ago. Let's go. I don't want to get caught in here." Izzy began to hurry toward the exit, fear rippling along her spine like a— She felt a tickle on her forearm and looked down; a hairy black spider crept toward her wrist. She jumped backward and brushed wildly at her arm as a stifled screech escaped her throat and the flashlight flew out of her hands. It hit the floor with a crack and went dark.

"Fantastic." Shelly sucked in a breath between clenched teeth. "What the heck were you doing?"

"There was a spider. On my arm." Izzy took several gulps of air, the weight of the unbroken darkness suddenly very oppressive.

"It's dark as a tomb in here."

"If you don't have anything nice to say, don't say anything at all," Izzy hissed.

"Sorry. Where are you? I can't stand to be in this total blackness all alone."

"Over here." Izzy waved her hands in front of her and collided with Shelly, who was doing the same thing.

Shelly gripped Izzy's arm with both hands. "How are we supposed to get out when we can't see anything?"

"Just stick one hand out until you touch the wall, then we'll follow it all the way back."

"*You* stick one hand out. You're the one who broke the flashlight."

Izzy made a squeaking noise. "I hate spiders." At the thought of more spiders dangling in the air around them, a shudder ripped through her.

"I am…relaxed," Shelly said softly. She drew a quick breath. "I am…relaxed. I am relaxed."

"What are you doing?"

"The walls are pressing in on me."

"Are you claustrophobic or something?"

"Yeah."

"You're claustrophobic? What were you doing insisting that we go into this tunnel?" Izzy slapped her friend's hand hard.

"I'm usually okay as long as there's light."

"Well, there isn't any."

"You don't have to rub it in." Shelly inhaled slowly. "I am…relaxed," she chanted. "I am relaxed."

"Stop it!"

"I can't stop it. Otherwise I freeze. I won't be able to move."

"I'm half-inclined to leave you in here forever." Izzy felt a fluttering on the back of her hand and jumped, squelching a scream. "Okay, we're getting out of here right now. Stick out your hand. We're going to move sideways until you make contact with the wall."

She shuffled them sideways as Shelly kept repeating, "I am…relaxed."

After a moment, Shelly said, "I'm touching the wall."

"Now all we have to do is move forward, one step at a time until we're out."

"What about the flashlight?"

"I'm not crawling around on this floor in the dark to find a broken light." Tugging Shelly forward, she began to move them down the tunnel. Five minutes later, hearts pounding, they stumbled back into the boathouse.

"Get me out of here," Shelly said on a gasp. She shoved the tunnel door closed just as Izzy opened the outside door. Bright morning light flooded the room and Shelly fled into it, laughing with such giddy delight, Izzy could have sworn she'd been rescued from a week in a collapsed mine shaft.

She rehung the oars and life jackets, making sure there was no sign that anyone had gone into the tunnel. No reason to advertise they'd been exploring where they didn't belong. Stopping in the boathouse doorway, she waved to the Steinmetzes. "Neat as a pin in here now," she called. She closed her eyes and let the morning sun warm her face. Hopefully they hadn't paid attention to how long she'd been in the boathouse—or wondered where Shelly had come from.

"Morning, Izzy."

At the sound of Gib's voice, her heart tripped and her eyes flew open. *I am…relaxed,* she said to herself. "Were you out fishing?"

He nodded. "Don't tell me you two are going out on the water. You could have come with me."

"Um, no, we were talking about it, but then we decided not to. I was making sure there were life jackets and oars in case—" She forced herself to stop.

"What's with her?" He eyed Shelly standing on the end of the dock, face raised upward, arms outstretched to the sky as if embracing the wide-openness of the world.

Izzy stepped onto the sand, shut the door behind her and said the first thing that popped into her head. "Morning nature-bonding ritual. A yoga thing that she does every day." She groaned inwardly; Gib was down here every morning to fish; he would have noticed Shelly before now. "This is her first time doing it at the beach."

"Is it relaxing?"

"Very. She swears by it." She felt a trickle of nervous sweat run between her shoulder blades.

Shelly strolled down the pier toward them, her expression one of absolute bliss.

"You ever do it?"

"No. I always meant to, but…"

"Maybe it would help me sleep at night. We should try it."

We?

When Shelly got closer, Gib asked, "Mind if I join you tomorrow morning?"

She slowed her steps and blinked. Izzy gestured loosely with her hands. "I told him about your morning nature-bonding ritual. The one you do every day."

"Ooh. Sure." Then, as if realizing she sounded less than convincing, Shelly said, "It really revs you up."

"I thought it was relaxing," Gib said.

"It relaxes and revs all at once," Izzy said hastily. "So you're ready for the day with energy—"

"*Calm* energy," Shelly interjected.

"Sounds intriguing. What time should I be here?"
Izzy swallowed.

"How about seven?" Shelly said.

"Seven it is." His gray eyes met Izzy's, and she had

the unsettling feeling that he could see directly through them into her soul. "You're coming, too, aren't you?"

She glanced away. She shouldn't. She really shouldn't spend more time with Gib Murphy—it muddled up her mind when she was trying to stay focused on her new career path. Besides, the more they were together, the more likely she or Shelly would make a slip and he'd discover her parents owned the land. No, she most definitely shouldn't come down here to-morrow morning. She looked him right in the eye. "I wouldn't miss it."

BOTTLE OF BEER IN HAND, Gib lay in a hammock at the beach later that day, taking a break after priming the freshly scraped exterior trim at Hickory Hollow. With any luck, he could get in a half hour's catnap before the primer was dry enough to be painted.

He took a drink of beer and watched the plump white clouds waft through the flawless blue sky. In the back-ground, he could hear the soothing lap of water against the sandy shore. If he didn't turn his head, he could almost pretend he was at an all-inclusive resort—not in northern Wisconsin, but on a Caribbean island, alone in paradise.

He brought the bottle to his mouth again and took a swallow. Nah, there he'd be drinking a mai tai or some-thing exotic. A waiter would be refilling his glass every time it even came close to being empty. And beauties in bikinis would be strolling the water's edge.

He closed his eyes. There was, of course, always the possibility he could be lucky here at White Bear. Maybe Izzy would decide to go for a swim—or at least a stroll in her swimsuit. Come to think of it, he hadn't seen her in a swimsuit yet—maybe she had a bikini. Maybe fortune would make her stroll by in it right now.

What did he have to lose by looking?

Opening one eye, he twisted his head slowly to the right and scanned the beach. Huh. The only view was Mrs. Steinmetz in a black one-piece almost-turtleneck swimsuit, sitting beside her husband in the shade of an ancient maple tree. No good luck that way.

He rolled his head the other direction and opened his right eye. No bikini girls this way, either. Just four kids leaping off the pier. Rascal wandered out of the woods to lick the hand Gib dangled off the side of the hammock, then dropped to the sand for a nap in the sun.

He should have known better than to expect anything exciting on White Bear beach. Finishing off his beer, he leaned down to stick the empty bottle in the sand.

"Gib Murphy?"

He looked up into the face of an early-forty-something businessman. Clean-shaven, white shirt, loose-knotted tie, sleeves cuffed up twice, no coat. The man smiled, showing off straight white teeth. Not their average guest. Still… "Yes?"

"I'm Jack Taylor of Taylor Development out of Milwaukee." He extended a hand. "We specialize in high-end condominium projects. They told me at the lodge you're the person I need to talk to."

"About what?"

"The land."

Gib spun off the hammock and onto his feet. "What about it?" he asked, leading Taylor away from the beach so they couldn't be overheard by the Steinmetzes. Who was this guy and what did he want? "What about the land?" he repeated when they were far enough away.

"Is there somewhere we can talk? I have some information you might find interesting."

So much for escaping to an exotic Caribbean beach. Gib narrowed his eyes. They couldn't talk in the lodge. Whatever this guy wanted to discuss, there was no reason to draw his grandparents into a conversation that may not accomplish anything except to upset them. "Yeah, follow me." He took one of the paths into the woods and unlocked an unrented cottage.

As Jack settled onto the faded tan sofa, Gib leaned against the kitchen doorjamb and crossed his arms over his chest. "I assume you know we don't own the land."

Jack leaned forward, elbows on his knees, hands clasped together. "I also know your lease gives you the right to match any legitimate offer the landowner gets."

Nothing new there. Gib eyed the patterned avocado-green linoleum in the kitchen with its worn-in traffic pattern. Jeez, but these places needed to be brought out of the sixties and seventies. "Yeah. So?"

"I hope I'm not talking out of school, but I understand you're having trouble securing the funds to match the offer they've received."

Where'd this guy say he was from? Milwaukee? Word sure got around fast. "Go on."

"Let's suppose you—the resort—was owned by partners. If you had a partner who could buy the land, you wouldn't have to lose the resort."

Interesting. "Are you saying you would be that partner?"

"My company is in excellent financial condition. I can

get a loan to buy the land, like this." He snapped his fingers. "We work together and you wouldn't lose the resort."

Gib eyed Jack's expensive shirt, his tailored pants, his probably Italian leather shoes. Why would a complete stranger care whether the Murphys were able to keep the resort? "What's in it for you?"

"Have a seat and I'll explain." Jack waved a hand at the green overstuffed chair opposite him and waited for Gib to sit down. "This is a terrific piece of property. Unfortunately, it never went on the market. The owners got an offer they like without ever listing the property." He steepled his fingers. "To be perfectly frank, I want this land. But the only way I can get it now is if I own the resort—as your partner."

Gib shook his head. "If you get the land, how does that help us keep the resort?"

"We draw up an agreement that your family can run the resort as long as they like. The acreage your buildings sit on wouldn't be developed and your guests would have beach access for as long as White Bear is open."

Gib considered Jack's proposal. It was definitely something none of them even thought about before. And it would enable his grandparents and Matt to stay on at the resort. Hell, this idea just might work. "Let me make sure I've got this straight. We take you on as a partner. You get first dibs to buy the land. Then my grandparents and brother can keep running the resort as long as they like."

"That's right."

"I have to admit, it has potential. Let me talk to my

grandparents and see what they think." He went over to the front window to gaze out at the woods. "What do you plan to do with the rest of the land?"

"A resort, condos and rentals, lakefront views. No roughing it—an upscale-vacation type of place."

"Restaurant?"

"Casual, but excellent food."

Gib cringed at the thought of this property all built up. The woods he and Matt had played in and explored as kids, cleared away, a few trees spared so they could provide shade for privately owned condo patios. "Swimming pool?" he asked, already knowing the answer.

"It's expected these days."

He didn't want to be here when this thing came to pass. White Bear's tiny log cottages would be like the wrong side of the tracks next to a big, shiny new neighbor. "I'll talk to the rest of the family and get back to you." He headed for the door, unable to shake the feeling that a front had blown in on this beautiful August day, and he wasn't sure there was anything he could do about it.

CHAPTER NINE

"WAKE UP." IZZY JOSTLED Shelly's shoulder the next morning. "It's our fifth day already and there's lots to do."

"Wh-what?" Shelly pulled the covers off her head and cracked open one eye to peer at the clock. "Why are you waking me up so early?" she mumbled.

"Because you told Gib he could join you for your nature-bonding ritual. And it's almost time." Izzy set a cup of coffee on the nightstand inches from Shelly's face. She hadn't seen Gib since yesterday morning, and much as she was trying to control her attraction to him, her stomach was fluttering with excitement.

"I wouldn't have said that if you hadn't told him I have a stupid ritual in the first place. Why didn't you tell him I was stretching?"

"My brain was still recovering from our escape out of spider haven." Izzy pulled open the curtains to brighten the room. "If you hadn't gone bananas once you got in the sun, we wouldn't be in this mess. Hurry up, it's a beautiful day."

Shelly creaked out of bed and eyed Izzy grumpily. "What's up with you, Miss Morning Sunshine? Cute shorts, cute top, cute hair, sparkly personality. Oh, wait,

I get it." She bobbed her head knowingly. "Of course. Beautiful Boy is going to be there."

"I always look like this."

Shelly snorted. "Whatever. So what do I do for a ritual?"

"Anything you want. Just make it believable." Izzy pointed at the alarm clock. "Hurry up or Gib might think we're not coming."

"I thought this wasn't about Gib, Miss I-look-like-a-million-bucks-all-the-time." Shelly pulled on the same clothes she'd been wearing yesterday, and they reached the beach only five minutes late.

Gib met them at the end of the trail, exceptionally adorable in his T-shirt and shorts, the epitome of rugged casual. "Morning. I was afraid you might not be coming."

"Not a chance," Shelly said. "I hate missing my nature…" She glanced at Izzy.

"Bonding ritual," Izzy finished cheerily, trying to appear as though she weren't compensating for Shelly's lapse.

"I'm here to greet the day, become one with nature." Gib stepped into the sun and opened his arms expansively. "What do we do first?"

"Follow me." Shelly straightened her shoulders and began to walk like a ballerina, toes pointed outward, stopping every four steps to plié.

"Is she serious?" Gib nodded at Shelly.

"I told you, she swears by it," Izzy said.

Shrugging, Gib said, "Well, okay. I'll give it a shot."

They fell into line behind Shelly, who suddenly began leaping gazellelike in large circles over the sand. Gib hesitated a second then followed, gamely springing across the beach. Izzy swallowed a laugh. She thought to herself that Andrew would never have stooped to such indecorous behavior, and it made her like Gib all the more.

Just when Izzy thought she couldn't hold it together another second, Shelly stopped and faced the lake, hands together in prayer position. She bowed toward the morning sun. "Everything we do has meaning," she said as Izzy and Gib followed suit. "With this, we pay tribute to the peacefulness of the day. Now, grasp the hand of the person next to you and bring your right hand to your heart."

"What does this mean?" Gib took Izzy's hand and squeezed it playfully. Warmth spread through her and she had to force herself to concentrate on Shelly's reply.

"It's symbolic of the connection between us all. Friends, families, *lovers.*"

Izzy threw a warning glare at Shelly, who replied with a serene nod, as if she was now in the self-fulfilled state of a yogi master or something.

"Still holding hands," Shelly said, "everyone reach for the sky. This is symbolic of our connection to the universe, the circle of life that makes us one with each other." Shelly brought her arms to her sides and started to turn in a circle. "Spin, spin," she said. "In this way we send our personal energy into the world."

This was bordering on ridiculous. Any minute, Gib was surely going to call them out.

"Turn and repeat after me. The day is mine, the day is yours."

When neither of them said anything, Shelly sighed. "We're almost done," she said. "Please."

"The day is mine. The days is yours," they repeated as they spun in circles. When his back was to Shelly, Gib made a face at Izzy. Hysteria bubbled up inside her and she broke eye contact to keep herself from doubling over.

"True goodness awaits," Shelly droned. "I will embrace the wholeness of the day. I will put aside my angers, fears, hatreds and insecurities. I will be pure and light and truth."

Izzy watched her, awestruck. All those years as a weather girl must have really honed her acting skills. They followed her, ballet-style, to the end of the pier and copied her as she thrust her arms upward and closed her eyes.

After a long minute of silence, her arms weakening, Izzy cracked open one eye and elbowed Shelly in the ribs.

"That's almost all for today," Shelly said so calmly Izzy could have sworn she'd taken a tranquilizer. "Now, sit on the end of the dock, cross-legged, holding hands."

"Seriously?" Izzy asked.

"Sit," Shelly commanded. "Because this is your first time, you must stay seated fifteen minutes feeling the karma flow in and out and around both of you. Then you can come up to the lodge for breakfast, which should consist only of plain oatmeal and dry toast."

Izzy opened her mouth to protest, but Shelly was already striding away down the dock.

"What are you people doing down here?" Mrs. Steinmetz asked from somewhere behind them.

"Bonding with nature," Shelly said pleasantly. "Getting in touch with our inner and outer karma."

"I love that sort of thing. Can I join you tomorrow?"

Seated at the end of the dock, Izzy looked back to see Shelly tilt her head in contemplation. "Absolutely. The more the merrier. Just be down here at seven. Barefoot."

"I'll tell Melvin. This would be beneficial for him, too."

Gib took Izzy's hand in his and they sat together in silence for several minutes, the moment so comfortable, she almost wished it would never end.

"So, it's all about karma," he said quietly. "I've never known what to think about the belief that our past actions create our future happiness or misery. Is it karma that brings people together? Or tears them apart? Is it karma that makes one business succeed while another fails? Lets one person live when another dies? Is it karma? Or is it just plain old luck?"

She didn't know how to answer. The wounds he was harboring were deep, his bitterness strong. He didn't need any more pain. Especially not from the woman whose family was responsible for a lot of the stress he was feeling. Much as she liked Gib Murphy, the best thing for both of them would be if she kept her distance. Because if he ever learned the truth, she might be the straw that broke him. She let go of his hand and got to her feet. "Let's go get our oatmeal."

GIB THREW THE BIG CANVAS drop cloth over the few pieces of furniture they had decided to keep in Hickory Hollow. "Painting the exterior went better than I expected yesterday," he said to Matt. "Let's hope this interior work is as easy."

Matt grumbled something unintelligible, and Gib didn't bother to ask him to repeat himself. He knew his brother disliked maintenance work. He never used to like it, either, but for some reason, he was getting a perverse satisfaction from working on this cottage. Maybe, as Shelly would say, it was good karma.

Matt knelt to stir a can of pale blue wall paint. "I can't see any of this making a difference. All this work and—"

"We don't have a choice. As soon as we get this cottage finished, we can shoot some photos and use them for the new Web site and brochure. The designer said he should have a preliminary layout—"

"So we can get the loan and keep the resort," Matt said as though speaking by rote. "Are you sure this is what you want?"

Gib raised his eyebrows. "What I want? I'm doing this for you and the grandparents. Once we get things headed in the right direction, you and Grampa can take over again."

Matt sat back on his haunches and eyed his brother.

"What?" Gib asked. He bent to wipe the dust off the dingy white baseboards.

"I'm not staying."

"Not staying where?"

"Here. I'm not staying. When you finish your manager stint, I'm done, too." Matt stood. "I'm leaving in October for Montana. Already got a job lined up in Big Sky. And I'm volunteering for ski patrol, too."

Gib straightened quickly. "Holy shit. When did this come about?"

"It's been coming about for a long time." Matt held up a hand. "And I'm sick of no one believing me. Two years ago I told the grandparents I was *thinking* about Montana, and they brought up how much they miss Mom and Dad. And how you were far away in war zones shooting pictures. And how they were so happy I didn't have the need for adventure like Mom and Dad used to have. And you, too. I didn't want to hurt them, so I buried it."

Gib knew exactly what was coming next. He remembered feeling the same way when he left White Bear.

"Now it's two years later and nothing's changed except things have gotten even more boring around here. The world's still passing me by."

"It just feels like that. Believe me, you're not missing that much." Gib taped off a window with blue painter's tape.

"Easy for you to say. You, who have been all over the planet already."

"I *am* eight years older."

Matt exhaled. "That's right. And in eight years, we can talk about it again, and maybe I'll have a different point of view." He slapped a dry paintbrush against the palm of his hand. "When you refused to stay after college, that was all right by me. I knew you wanted to see the world. But then, suddenly, everyone was expecting me to be the heir apparent. And I don't want to be. *I'm going to Big Sky.*"

Gib stared at his younger brother a long minute as he frantically scrambled for some coherent thing to say. "Jeez, Matt, I thought you loved it here. That this was, like, your dream life. All the outdoors."

"Some of it is. The woods. The lake. The skiing. I *hate* the resort. If anyone should understand, I'd think it would be you. Once you got out, you hardly ever came home again."

Well, yeah… "But I was always halfway around the world. Not exactly close enough for weekend visits."

"You're not fooling me. You didn't want to get roped into working here again."

"Wow." He could hardly believe it. Matt wanted out and, until this moment, Gib hadn't had a clue. How had he gotten so out of touch with his own brother? He taped off another window and started on the baseboard.

"That's all you have to say? *Wow?*"

"I'll have a lot more to say once I decide what it is and how to say it," Gib said. His brother seemed so young. He wanted to ask *what's the rush?* but knew that would come right back in his face. "Obviously the grandparents don't know."

"If they'd pay attention, *ever,* they might figure it out. But, no, I haven't told them. I was leaning toward not telling anyone until I packed my car and drove away."

"Oh, that would be sweet."

"I don't want them to be looking at me with sad faces for months. You need to understand—*I'm out of here in October.*" Matt's voice was solid determination.

"I get it. And, believe it or not, I understand. Completely. So, you think Grandma and Grampa can handle this place alone?"

"Don't try to guilt me," Matt said, holding both hands up as though holding back Gib's words. "I feel bad enough already."

"I'm not. You've been here, I haven't. But, Matt, let's face the facts. You don't want this place. I don't want it. The grandparents are seventy. Realistically, how much longer can they keep going at this?"

Matt shrugged. "I don't think they have a choice. All they have is this resort—no money."

Gib tore another piece of blue tape off the roll and pressed it down on the baseboard. What a frickin' roller coaster. After meeting with that developer yesterday, he'd decided to put off any decisions until he knew for sure that the family wouldn't qualify for the loan on their own. No reason to take on a partner if they didn't need one. But now, with Matt wanting out…hell… "You think your leaving will change the grandparents' minds about wanting to buy the land?" He knew the answer before Matt even said anything.

"Are you kidding? Grandpa always says he was born here and he's going to die here. They've been running the place for forty years—I'd say they're set in their life-style by now."

"So you think retirement would be a no-go even if they had some money?"

"Those two?" Matt spread a drop cloth on the floor along the wall. "Like I said, they *live* for this resort. It would about kill them to leave it behind."

"That's what I thought. Problem is, if neither of us is going to be here to help and we succeed in getting the loan for the land—"

"How are they going to run the resort?"

"Yeah."

Matt pushed the drop cloth into the corner. "Hire more help, I guess. You know how much I love them—they're like our parents. But I *have* to go, no matter how much they want me to stay."

"Ah, the impatience of youth—"

"Like you're an old man."

"Lately, I've been feeling like one. You know, the grandparents are just afraid something will happen to you. Like it did to Mom and Dad…" *And almost to me.*

"Yeah, and I'm afraid *nothing* will happen to me. That's an even worse prospect."

Gib remembered feeling exactly the same way once. He opened the old wooden ladder and positioned it near a window as he considered Matt's announcement and the discussion he'd had yesterday with Jack Taylor.

This latest development didn't change anything. Not really. His grandparents would still want to buy the land. And Gib still wouldn't be able to live with himself if he didn't do everything he could to help them get the loan. Until that avenue closed, Taylor's proposal had to stay on the back burner. "Don't say anything to Grandma and Grampa for a while. Let's get this cottage finished, the Web site designed and up, the brochure done. Then let me talk to the bank again. If they refuse us the loan, your leaving will be a nonissue. Because, one way or another, everything's going to change."

IZZY OPENED THE WISCONSIN map on the old oak front desk and smoothed out the folds, rotating it right side up for Gib's grandfather.

"All righty, then," he said. "Let me see. 'Course, there's the well-known places where Dillinger and Capone and some of those big-name gangsters used to stay. Manitowish Waters, that's where the big Dillinger shoot-out was. But there's less-known spots, too. Near as I remember, there's quite a few around here with stories of their own." He ran a finger along a road on the map. "You know, hardly anyone knows Capone stayed here at our place for years before he built his hideout in Couderay. My granddad said he modeled his lodge after White Bear. 'Course, he could have been making that up to impress us kids." He took a pen and paper from the drawer. "Anyhow, you want to know where some of those less-known places are?"

"I think it would add perspective," Izzy said. "Can you give us directions?"

He blew out a breath. "All those little back roads… and some are under construction. Even with directions, you're likely to get lost. More than once." He pushed open the front door and shouted for Gib, waving him in. Izzy felt her face flush and she bent toward the map.

"The girls want to do some filming over in Woodruff, Minocqua, Manitowish Waters," Pete said. "You know, seems to me I heard the Capone mob ran a crime school in Hurley during the twenties. That's quite a haul from here, though." He eyed Gib's paint-splattered T-shirt and shorts. "I'm thinking someone should go with them so they don't get lost on the back roads. I would, but I've got, well, some business in town."

Gib gave his grandfather a reproachful look. Izzy felt Shelly's elbow in her ribs and muttered, "Tupperware," in reply.

"You want to go with these two and help them out?"

Izzy cringed. If she was going to stay away from Gib, spending the afternoon together wasn't a step in the right direction. "Oh, you don't have to come along," she said hurriedly. "I'm sure we can find—"

"Pete's right," Gib said. "It'll be way easier if you have someone along who knows the roads around here."

"But you're in the middle of painting."

"I'm waiting for the walls to dry so I can do the trim. Let me change clothes."

Three hours later, after shooting footage at a couple of other locations, they were interviewing the owner of a supper club who was describing how Baby Face Nelson used to sit at the end of the restaurant's bar, his back always to the wall. Then he took them outside and showed them the dip in the back driveway where Dillinger reputedly spun out his car before taking to the woods on foot during an escape from the feds.

"Our resort was never owned by gangsters, but they did like to stay here," the man continued, warming to the topic. "Come down by the water and I'll show you where they used to store the whiskey they brought in from Canada." He headed toward the beach with Shelly right behind him.

Izzy touched Gib on the arm and hung back to let the others go ahead. "This is the third place today and the story is the same," Izzy whispered. "Well, not exactly the same, but, close enough. What gives?"

"There were a lot of gangsters vacationing up here during Prohibition. Most stayed at existing resorts, so every bar owner can tell you where these guys ate and drank."

"Even if they never did."

"Exactly."

They caught up to the other two and Izzy set down the tripod and continued filming.

"This used to be quite a big building." The owner

pointed to the remnants of a stone foundation, long overgrown. "Back in '33, Frankie Marone holed up here late one night. He'd been in a feud with a rival Chicago gang for a couple of years and the fight moved to Wisconsin. Frankie and his men were outnumbered, so they headed for the beach where they had a powerboat. They only made it this far before they had to take cover inside."

The man strolled around the foundation perimeter. "There was a shoot-out. Then an explosion. This building went up like a fireball and that was it. Frankie and the men with him, all dead." He stepped through the opening in the foundation that had once been a doorway. "Turns out the whole thing was a setup. The building had been rigged with explosives. Frankie had been *allowed* to escape this far so he and his men could be disposed of with no witnesses, no bodies."

Izzy shivered and glanced at Gib. His face was white. "Are you okay?" she asked quietly.

"I, uh…yeah." He turned and walked down the beach.

She watched him uncertainly, then stepped back from the camera and said to Shelly, "Keep filming. I'll be right back." She followed Gib for a minute, quickening her pace so she could fall into step beside him. He glanced at her, brow furrowed.

"No one should ever look that alone," she said in answer to his unspoken question. "I didn't want you to be."

They walked in silence for another couple of minutes.

"I guess I should explain," he finally said.

"You don't have to."

"I know." The shade of a nearby tree cast a dark shadow over his face. "But I want to. I want you to know. There was a hotel I always stayed at in Iraq. Lots of journalists, photographers—the media—we all stayed there. It had reinforced concrete barriers, was well guarded."

"A safe place." Izzy felt dread wash through her as though she was about to hear a horror story that she already knew. She'd read stories like this in the paper, heard them on the nightly news.

"It was a haven where you could relax, let your guard down. We should have been safely up in our rooms when it happened. Would have been if…" He looked out into the distance. "There were five of us. We were out chasing down the story of another bombing. The other guys wanted to take off, but I kept shooting pictures. Kept thinking that I hadn't caught what I wanted on film yet. Photojournalists…the pictures we shoot tell a story, answer the question—what happened? I heard someone once say, *We shoot verbs—not nouns.*"

He exhaled sharply. "If I'd quit ten minutes earlier. *Five minutes earlier.* If I hadn't gone along. If only I'd said, 'Let's stop and get something to eat before we go back to the hotel.'" His voice cracked. "If only…"

Izzy took his hand in hers. "You couldn't have known."

"The guy drove a truck full of explosives into the barrier at the hotel. There was no logic in it—no way was he going to penetrate that concrete wall. It happened as we were crossing the street. We saw him coming and started to run. There were five of us… Did I say that yet?"

"Five of you," she said past the knot in her throat.

"Four took shrapnel and Dave didn't get hurt at all except where his arms got skinned when he fell…" He clenched his teeth together and a muscle tightened in his jaw. "When I got off the ground, Chris was dead. Alex died on the way to the hospital. Terry a couple of days later. Me? The worst I got was in the knee."

He bent to pick up a handful of sand and let it run through his fingers. "Just like this, lives disappeared. Just like this, they're gone. They died and I lived. They should have been safely inside the hotel, except they waited for me."

She could hear his guilt. And regret. "It wasn't your fault. Anything can happen, anywhere. All of us could spend a lifetime second-guessing decisions, places, times—"

"It should have been me. The guys were always razzing me about wanting the perfect shot. And they were right. I did. They died because I had to stay a few more minutes to capture the despair of those people on film, their horror at having survived something that their friends didn't." He rubbed the back of his hand on his jaw. "Pretty ironic. I didn't get the shot I wanted, but I got to know what they feel. I know the despair. And I relive it every time I close my eyes."

Izzy's heart lurched. She wished she knew how to take his pain away. She reached up to cup his face in her hands and force him to look at her. "Listen to me. It's not your fault. Terrible things happen. They're supposed to happen to other people, but sometimes the other people are *us*." She could hardly stand the emptiness in his eyes.

Without warning, he crushed her against him and took her mouth hard, as if she was the air he needed to stay alive. He cupped her head in his hands and laced his fingers through her hair, and though she knew she should push away, knew that no good could come of this, she gave herself up to him and kissed him back. Her heart pounded and her knees weakened and she grabbed hold of his shirt in both hands to keep herself from collapsing. Behind her closed eyelids, the bright sun sparkled like fireworks, and she thought to herself that Gib felt so right. His hands skimmed down her back and under the hem of her T-shirt, and she let herself spin dizzily into the heat of him. When finally he broke the kiss, she was breathless and dazed.

"We'd better go back." He looked as stunned as she felt.

She touched a hand to her mouth. Go back to what? Gib Murphy had just ensured she could never return to the way things had been with him before. And with devastating clarity she knew better than to even think about moving forward with him.

CHAPTER TEN

THE PHONE CALL CAME IN at exactly ten o'clock that night, right after the day had gone still and the sun had set. Gib took the receiver from his grandfather and listened in stunned disbelief to the shaking voice of the middle-aged man on the other end of the line. Dave was dead. Dave, the only one of them who'd managed to get through the explosion unscathed. He'd taken a curve on his motorcycle late the night before and lost control. On a road he'd been down a thousand times before.

Gib cursed. "Why? He came home whole…and then this?" Except, inside he knew after everything they'd been through, Dave, like him, was only whole on the outside. He asked a few questions, searching for a reason, hoping to learn the purpose of this tragedy. Finally, numb, he expressed his regrets and sympathies and set down the phone.

"What happened?" his grandfather asked.

"Another friend. A journalist…motorcycle accident. I've gotta get outside." He went to the beach in the dark, to the end of the pier, and curled his bare toes over the wooden edge. Staring into the black water, he tried to picture what it felt like to hurt so much you wanted to die.

Ah, but he knew. Or very nearly did. He just buried it, shoved it away, refused to acknowledge its existence so he could keep functioning. As the thought peeled away the fragile cover from his own pain, anger exploded within him. His fury grew, blocking out everything until all he could feel was raw emotion and the frustration that there was nothing he could do to change anything that had happened. He spun round and headed toward the lodge, unable to stay still, feeling like if he didn't do something he would implode.

He flipped on the light outside the shed, got out the wood-splitting maul and set a log on the chopping block. This was for Dave. And for Terry and Chris and Alex. He positioned his feet shoulder-width apart and gripped the handle firmly with both hands, as though doing this very correctly would somehow fix everything. Then he swung hard into the wood and split the log. He picked up half and split it once more.

Log after log, fury driving each stroke, he split wood until sweat ran in rivulets down his back, drenching his shirt. "Dammit, Dave. What the hell were you doing?" His breathing came hard and he swore again and again, the sound of the maul hitting the wood like an exclamation point on his curses. "You should have called me. I thought you were okay."

Sweat ran into his eyes and he wiped a hand across them to clear his vision. He swung again and the bit sank into the wood and stuck. "Shit." He yanked at the maul, twisted the handle hard. "You should have called me. Dammit, you should have—" He rocked the handle to free the maul. "Aw, Dave—what were you thinking… What—" Suddenly, the bit wrenched loose and he jerked upright, almost losing his balance. Tears blended with perspiration to blur his sight once more. He swung forcefully again, as if the harder he worked the more he could hold back the pain trying to claw its way out from inside him.

Dave had survived, had gone home to take a vacation, escape the horror for a while. And now, for him, the horror was gone forever. And so was the laughter and the friendship…and the beers they shared after filing their stories and sending their photos…and the world problems they'd solved over those beers… and the women they'd chased…and the dreams they'd compared…and the hopes they'd both had…

Dave was dead and Gib couldn't change it.

Chopping all the wood in the world wouldn't make a difference. Shoulders sagging, he went inside to change his shirt. He didn't even want to try to sleep tonight, knew that if sleep came at all, it would be tortured. What was the purpose in all this? What was the point in working so hard to make things good when, in a second, everything could be destroyed, futures gone, lives lost?

He took the path to Hickory Hollow, dug his keys from his pocket and unlocked the door. They were almost finished here. Just some painting left to do and their showcase cottage would be ready for unveiling.

And for what? To try to save this damn resort so they could work themselves to death waiting on people? His brother had already made it clear he wanted out. His grandparents…they couldn't keep going at this pace. Why hadn't they sold White Bear years ago when the lease still had decades left on it?

He shook his head at the stupidity of the question. Because they loved this place; they didn't want to leave. And now, here he was trying to get the land for them so they could stay. So he could get back to life as he knew it, being so busy there wasn't even time to think about death.

Until it smacked him upside the head.

He picked up the paintbrush from the drop cloth on the floor and pressed the bristles against the palm of his opposite hand, squeezing the handle hard as anger and hatred coursed through him. Chris and Terry and Alex had died. And now Dave. A moan escaped from low in his throat.

He flipped on the radio and spun the dial until he found a radio talk show, some woman discussing azalea bushes and how they needed to be protected from cold and wind. Good advice—if only he'd been able to do it for his friends. As the guest prattled on about providing windbreaks, he changed to a music station, then pried open the fresh can of paint and gave it a quick stir. The way he was feeling, he would probably be able to work all night without getting tired at all.

"WE LEFT THE FLASHLIGHT in the tunnel!" Izzy shot upright in her chair. She glanced at Shelly, sound asleep on the couch in front of the TV. "Shell, wake up! Shelly!"

Shelly startled awake and raised her head. "What? Why do you keep waking me up when I'm sound asleep?"

"We left the flashlight in the tunnel."

"Yeah, well, seems to me it was you who said we

weren't going to crawl around on the floor in pitch darkness to find it." Shelly let her head drop back against the couch. "Jeez, I'm exhausted. How could I have said I'd do that crack-of-dawn morning ritual thing again tomorrow?"

"It belonged in this cabin."

"I'll buy them a new one."

"Listen to me. *Beechwood,* the name of our cottage, was printed on the side in permanent marker."

Shelly rubbed both hands over her face and opened her eyes again. "So? The Murphys already said they never go in the tunnel."

"What if they're lying about that? They certainly were stretching the truth about the tunnel being clogged full of stuff. What if they're in there all the time? If I kept gambling records in my tunnel, I'd say it was impassable. too. Just to keep people out."

Shelly sat up slowly and grinned. "Wait. Are you thinking something illegal's going on around here? You're not joking? Because—"

"I don't know." Izzy paced the room and tried to organize her thoughts into coherency. "What if they are involved in something? With all the stuff they have down there…all those ledger books…they have to go into the tunnel once in while. What if there are other records down there—more current ones? What if they find the flashlight and discover we were in there when they expressly told us to *keep out* and then they think we were snooping around and know something that we don't actually know and—"

"And what if they're into organized crime?" Shelly made a slashing motion across her throat.

Izzy felt her eyes widen. "Oh, come on."

"Who knows? All that matters is you've convinced me we need to get that flashlight. But we're bringing two lights with us this time. I'm not risking a replay of our last escapade."

Fifteen minutes later they were standing in the shadows where the woods met the beach, eyeing the dark shape of the boathouse in the night.

"I'm starting to freak out about going in there again," Shelly said. "Let's hurry up." She pointed at the sky. "Those are cumulonimbus clouds coming our way. If I'm right, we're in for a serious thunderstorm—"

"You were predicting rain a couple of days ago and it didn't happen."

"Yeah, but that front is really close. Let's go."

They hurried down the beach, feet sinking into the soft sand with every step, the light of the moon enough to let them see without using a flashlight.

Once safely inside the boathouse, Shelly pried open the tunnel door. "I'll stand guard," she said. "You go get it."

"I'm not going in there alone."

"You know how those walls close in on me."

"We're not going to be in the dark this time," Izzy said. "If one flashlight goes out, we've got another. Come on."

"Fine. Lead on." Shelly followed Izzy into the tunnel, leaving the door open so they could make a quick exit. "What if they already found it?"

Izzy's stomach began to churn. "They couldn't have. Otherwise, they would have said something. Sweep that beam on the floor." Gingerly, they made their way along the passage. Finally, Izzy spotted the flashlight against the wall and swooped to pick it up. "Let's go."

"Shh." Shelly held a finger to her lips. She pointed at the ceiling.

Izzy cringed, half expecting to see an army of spiders or bats or centipedes above her. Then she heard the murmur of conversation.

"We must be in the section under the lodge. I think that's Pete and Catherine." Shelly cocked her head as if it would help her hear better.

Pieces of conversation slipped through.

"…said he was betting on the Packers…"

Catherine answered, "Still only the preseason…"

"After last year, the odds aren't…"

"What are they talking about?" Izzy whispered.

"Football."

Suddenly Catherine was almost directly above them. "We've got every record going back thirty years. I could show him exactly…"

Izzy tapped Shelly's arm, then hiked a thumb over her shoulder to say, let's get out of here, *now.* They hurried back through the tunnel. Only when they were back on the beach did she finally exhale in relief. "You know what? If the Murphys are into something, I don't want to know. I don't care what else is in that tunnel, I don't care what the family is up to, I'm never going in there again."

"Amen, sister, I'm with you there." Shelly fanned herself with both arms. "I love wide-open spaces. When is the last time you saw a view like this? Wide open for as far as the eye can see."

The lake stretched out before them, shimmering in

the moonlight, tall pines on the far shore stretching into the star-studded sky. Even with the dark line of a storm front on the horizon, the view was breathtaking. Izzy felt a twinge of wistfulness. "Paradise like this is getting hard to find."

"Might I point out that your family owns this piece of paradise?"

"What's that supposed to mean?"

Shelley set off toward their cottage. "If I had your parents' money, I wouldn't be in any big rush to sell this off. There's a way of life here that's disappearing. No worries except whether to swim, canoe or lie in the sun. The dinner bell rings at five. Breakfast made to order."

"Yeah," Izzy said thoughtfully. "All's right with the world." Doubts about her parents' decision began to cloud in her mind. Until this moment, she'd never fully appreciated what the Murphys had here and the magnitude of what they were losing.

Maybe she should talk to her folks about extending the lease. She shook her head. That would never be an option; her parents had been waiting for this lease to come due for years so they could end being landlords. The only way they'd ever consider working something out with the Murphys was if a land sale was involved.

"Check out Hickory Hollow." Shelly pointed at the cottage down another path, its every window aglow. "Lit up like the stage of a Broadway musical. Someone's afraid of the dark."

"That's the cabin they're remodeling." Izzy slapped a mosquito on the back of her hand. "The boys are probably working late." She wondered whether Gib was inside and mentally chastised herself for the thought.

"Maybe you should check on their progress. See if B.B. can paint as good as he looks," Shelly said with a smirk.

"Maybe we should both check."

"I was asleep until someone decided they wanted to go spelunking. I'd like to be asleep again. You go."

"Matt's probably in there, too." No way should she knock on that door.

Shelly sighed melodramatically and waved a dismissive hand. "If only he were ten years older. Go on. Don't stay out too late." She disappeared down the path, the faint light of her flashlight the only visible sign she was in the woods. And then even that was gone and Izzy was standing alone on the cottage stoop, her heart skipping every third beat. From inside came the sound of a radio DJ chatting away the night. She raised a hand to knock on the door then froze, her fist inches from the wood. This was ridiculous. Less than twenty-four hours after she decided she should keep her distance from Gib, she was knocking on his door? What did she think she was going to say once she got inside? *How's it going in here? That's a lovely paint color? Want to kiss me again?*

No, that last wasn't even an option. She dropped her hand and took several steps along the path before stopping. Gib did tell her to swing in if she saw them working, she rationalized. So, there really was nothing wrong with her saying hello. Just drop in for a howdy-doody, *guten abend,* what's shakin', aloha kind of thing.

That should be a hit.

Before she could waste another moment vacillating, she turned back to the door and rapped soundly, then stepped inside without waiting for a reply. The odor of wet paint hung in the air and music blasted from the boom box in the living room, but no one was around. She stuck her head through the open doorway of the nearest bedroom and spotted Gib up on a stepladder.

"Well, hello. What are you doing here?" he asked over the sound of the radio. Paintbrush in hand, he backed down the ladder.

"I was taking a walk," Izzy lied. "Saw the lights on and thought I'd see how things were going."

"They're going. Once I finish this room, we can start putting it all back together again. New curtains, some better furniture…"

"I like the color." Izzy studied the pale blue-gray wall he'd already finished.

He didn't reply and the silence stretched between them awkwardly, like a rubber band ready to break. She began to wish she hadn't stopped in.

"So, how's the filming coming along?" Gib finally asked.

"Good. We were reviewing some footage earlier tonight and it's…pretty good." Maybe she could research synonyms for *good* on the computer when she got back to her cottage.

"As long as White Bear Lodge comes off looking great."

She smiled. "I don't think you have to worry. Especially because the main focus is the gangsters and their holidays. How they lived…"

"And died," he said in a strangled voice.

"Well, no, we're not going to get into—" She broke off at the expression on Gib's face. "What's the matter?"

"Remember my friend, Dave, I told you about? He

died last night in a motorcycle accident," he said dully. "No helmet, dry pavement, no alcohol. Just a sharp curve taken too fast on a road he'd traveled many, many times before."

"No," Izzy whispered.

"He didn't come out of that explosion unhurt, after all." Gib stood there clutching a paintbrush in his left hand, his grief almost palpable.

Izzy's heart wrenched at the naked vulnerability on his face. "Oh, Gib. I'm so sorry." She searched for something to say that might help him, then realized it wasn't words he needed. Taking the brush from his hand, she set it across the top of the paint can. Then she wrapped her arms around him and held him close.

"I talked to him only once since I got back," he said against her hair. "I thought he was doing okay."

"You couldn't have known. You have your own things you're dealing with here."

In the background, the DJ blabbered on about a party he'd gone to last weekend, then put the next song into play, dedicated by some girl named Haley to her boyfriend. The strains of "My Heart Will Go On" filled the room. "Takes me back to high school," Gib said. "Once *Titanic* came out, the girls practically fainted whenever this song played."

He tightened his arms around her and began to sway with the music and she followed his lead. The haunting words and melody filled her with melancholy, a longing for all the hopes and dreams that were launched during those teenage years only to die a premature death.

"I bet they all wanted to dance with you." She wished the two of them were dancing right now because he wanted to dance with her and not because he needed the comfort of someone's arms around him.

She felt him chuckle.

"I'm sure there were plenty who couldn't have cared less," he said.

"Where did you grow up?"

He didn't answer right away. "We lived outside Madison until I was ten. Used to come up and stay here with my grandparents for a month every summer. Then my parents died in a small plane crash and Matt and I moved here permanently."

"I'm sorry." Her words felt so inadequate.

"They'd taken a trip, were going to hike up Mount Rainier to celebrate their anniversary. My grandma says they gave me my adventurous soul."

Izzy swallowed the lump in her throat. "I used to think things happened in life to teach you something. But the older I get, the more I wonder." The song ended and she stepped out of his arms, wanting to put some distance between them. She leaned against the doorjamb. "But what's a ten-year-old supposed to learn from his parents dying?"

Gib pulled the canvas drop cloth back from the end of the bed and sat down. "I've spent the past couple of hours trying to figure out what the point is, why some people die and some live. What's the meaning of life if you can't ever count on life to hang around as long as it's supposed to?"

If only she knew how to help him.

After a minute, Gib stood. "I'd better start painting again before my brush gets hard."

"It's almost midnight. Are you planning to stay up all night?"

"Probably."

"And then go fishing in the morning to get some sleep."

"You're catching on." His smile didn't reach his eyes. "It's easier, sometimes, to stay up."

"Maybe TV would help. It puts me to sleep fast enough." She didn't feel comfortable leaving him alone, not with all the jagged edges in his life right now.

"It's not the falling asleep that's the problem. It's the staying asleep. It's the dreams, the waking in the darkness disconcerted, disconnected and…" He shook his head. "Drenched in sweat like a kid having a nightmare. About monsters in the closet, under the bed, coming through the doorway. And nowhere to hide."

That settled it. She wasn't leaving him alone. She picked up the clean paint roller from the paint tray and held it up. "I've been told I'm one step away from professional," she exaggerated. "Must have been a skill I was born with. So…how about I lend you a hand?"

GIB FELT HIS MOOD LIGHTEN. As much as he wanted to be alone, he didn't want to be alone. "You sure?"

She nodded. "What else have I got to do?"

"Sleep."

"Had too much Coke with dinner. I'm not going to be sleeping anytime soon."

He felt absurdly happy that she'd insisted. "Okay, you're hired."

Two hours later, they finished the job amid spirited discussions about the state of the union, world politics, global warming, and which famous actor was dating which famous actress.

For a while, anyway, he forgot about death, forgot about life, forgot about everything but Izzy. He watched her as she rinsed the roller out in the kitchen sink and wished, just for tonight, he had someone to climb into bed with, someone to wrap his body around so that when the nightmares came, so, too, would come reassurance that everything was okay. God, now he sounded like a kid. He'd survived long nights alone before; he'd get through tonight.

Izzy went into the living room to peek out the window. "Looks like we never got the storm Shelly was predicting." She glanced at her watch and yawned. "Jeez, it's almost two."

"You'd better get home or you'll be exhausted tomorrow." Gib rinsed his paintbrush under the faucet. "Thanks for helping. And for keeping me company."

"Anytime. You going up to the lodge?" She picked up her flashlight and absently played with the on-off button as he walked her to the door.

"Yeah. As soon as I close this place up." With the windows open and the warm night air blowing in, the paint smell was already dissipating. No reason to go to the lodge right away—if at all. He shut the door behind her, stretched out on the brown plaid couch and began to channel-surf with the remote—a few minutes of CNN, an old black-and-white Jimmy Stewart movie, a little *South Park,* a reality dating show, an infomercial about skin care products—

"I thought you were going home," Izzy said.

He twisted around to see her in the doorway. Hell, he hadn't even heard the door open. "I am…eventually. Thought I'd do like you said and watch some TV."

"Until dawn?"

He ignored her and refocused his attention on the infomercial.

"Does anything help?"

"Nope."

She took the throw off the arm of the rocking chair, then snapped off the end table lamp. "Move over."

He didn't budge. "What?"

She sat on the edge of the couch and nudged him with an elbow. "Move over," she said more forcefully.

This time he did as he was told. She opened the throw and covered him, then slid beneath it, stretched out beside him on the couch, her back to his front. Reaching behind her, she took the remote from his hand and clicked the television off. Darkness engulfed them. "Now, go to sleep," she said.

He drew a breath, inhaled the scent of her, cocoa butter on her skin and lime in her hair. He wrapped his arm around her and nestled her into the curve of his body. Then he kissed the back of her neck, closed his eyes and surrendered to the exhaustion he'd been holding at bay.

EYES OPEN, IZZY LISTENED to the soft, steady rhythm of Gib's breathing and hoped he would be able to sleep until morning without any of the nightmares he'd become so accustomed to. She could only imagine his grief, the ache that must have begun when his parents died and only got worse with each friend's death. Add to that his fears about losing the resort that had been in his family for almost a century and it was no wonder he couldn't sleep at night.

She dreaded the day he learned her parents owned the land. The more she got to know him and his family, the heavier this secret weighed on her. Better that Gib Murphy never find out Izzy Stuart was really Elizabeth Gordon. That way, when she left here, they would remember each other as friends.

When she left here.

The thought bared a hollow spot in her chest, the way a chill wind skims the surface water off a lake. She closed her eyes against the feeling and forced herself to think about her documentary. About all the success she would find once she and Shelly finished production.

Somewhere deep inside, she could feel the hollow spot grow.

CHAPTER ELEVEN

A RIFLE CRACKED AND GIB startled to half-awake, every muscle tensed, ready for action. Where? It cracked again, sharp and clear, and he jerked, struggling to pull his mind to consciousness. Sniper. "Move! Get out of here!" he mumbled.

He felt a gentle hand on his forearm.

"It's a storm," a woman said in a voice soft with sleep.

He waited, confused. Into the silence came the splat of bullets against the roof, first only a few, then more and more. "We need to go—"

"It's just rain," she murmured, rubbing his arm. "Nothing to fear."

Rain? Slowly he came awake. He blinked his eyes open and focused. Izzy. He was with Izzy. He let himself relax against her. He was at home in Wisconsin. They were sleeping in the cottage. Iraq was half a world away. "We'd better close the windows."

"Did that an hour ago when the wind picked up," Izzy said.

Lightning cracked again, closer, almost directly overhead. It was a classic Midwestern summer storm, the kind he used to love as a kid. Thunder roared and wind rattled the windows.

"There's nothing like the sound of rain on the roof," Izzy murmured. "When I was young, I liked riding in the car in rainstorms at night. Especially when we were on a road trip. Made me feel protected."

Gib pushed up on one elbow. Her face was soft, flushed creamy pink with sleep, her eyes sultry under heavy lids. He almost kissed her but stopped himself, not wanting to make her uncomfortable when she had stayed out of concern for him. "I bet your parents didn't feel the same way about it."

"Yeah, now that I'm the driver, I hate being on the road in rainstorms."

"Where'd you grow up?"

"Down south." She rolled to sitting and looked at her watch, then showed it to him. "It's past seven-thirty—"

"I slept that long? It's so dark I didn't realize how late it was."

"Did you dream?"

He sat up beside her. "If I did, I don't remember it. Man, do I feel good. That's the best sleep I've had since…before I got back."

"I hope you're not supposed to be working the breakfast shift."

"No. I've got a meeting at the bank at nine-thirty."

"About the resort?" Izzy tossed off the blanket and stood, stretching to one side and then the other.

"That's all I meet about these days." Suddenly he missed her beside him, wished she could stay every night so he could feel this refreshed each morning. He swung his feet to the floor and went to the door to watch the storm. A driving wind whipped the tree branches and slapped the rain against the leaves. "I missed these storms when I was away."

Izzy joined him at the door. "I'd better get back before Shelly calls the police because I didn't come home last night. We're supposed to interview the owner of Lost Loon Resort later this morning." She put a hand on the doorknob.

"What time?" he asked, stalling so she didn't leave. He hadn't slept with a woman in a long time—sex or no sex—and he didn't want to lose the connection he felt with her.

"Supposed to be at ten, but with this rain, we'll probably have to reschedule." She twisted the knob and he took hold of her arm to stop her. She raised her face, lips softly parted in surprise. He knew he should let her go, but all he wanted right now was to take her back to the couch and make love to her.

AT THE EXPRESSION ON Gib's face, Izzy gently tugged her arm free, regret shading her thoughts. If only she'd met Gib Murphy under other circumstances. If only he already knew her parents owned the land. If only… Too many *if onlys*. She had to get out of here. "I have to go," she said softly, and let herself out of the cottage.

She welcomed the drenching rain, the cold that seeped beneath her skin to numb her growing feelings for Gib. Halfway to the cottage, she slipped on the woodsy path and landed on her knees in the mud. A sob escaped her throat and she held back the tears that threatened to follow. For the first time since arriving at White Bear, she wanted to leave. Wanted to run away from the monster that had been born the day she decided to come here. She got to her feet, hands now as muddy as her knees. There was no one to blame for this disaster but herself.

Reaching the cottage, she charged through the doorway, leaving a trail of mud. She stood on the mat inside the front door, shivering, water running off her legs and pooling at her feet.

"Nice to see you again." Shelly grabbed a bath towel and tossed it her way. "Have fun last night?"

Izzy draped the towel over her shoulders. "It's not what you think. A friend of his was killed yesterday." She told Shelly about the motorcycle accident. "It didn't seem right to leave him alone. Not with another friend dying." She went into the bathroom to take a shower and wash her hair, letting the hot water pound on her head until her skin began to prune. Then she got out and wrapped a clean towel around herself.

"We slept on the couch together," she said as she headed into her bedroom to get dressed. "Nothing else. But if he had made a move…" She felt a twinge. "It would have taken every ounce of self-control to say no. And even then I don't think I would have. It isn't that I don't know all the dangers and pitfalls of getting involved with Gib… But even when I tell myself we have a movie to make, new careers to chase down, that he's going to the other side of the world to shoot pictures again, that I'm Elizabeth Gordon and my parents are selling the land his family wants…it's like, I ignore all of that. When I'm with him, all I want is to be with him. Even if all I can have is a moment. Do I sound nuts?"

"No. Does he want it, too?"

She remembered the desire on Gib's face this

morning, his hand on her arm. "I think so. But he's dealing with so many issues. And if we get involved, it's inevitable that he'll find out who I am. *I'll have to tell him.* I can't see that information doing anything except causing more pain." She regarded herself in the dresser mirror and ran a brush through her wet hair. "I won't do that to him."

"Here's a novel idea. Why don't you find a way for the Murphys to get the land? Then Gib'll be happy because the family keeps the resort, you'll be happy because you helped them keep the resort, and the two of you can be happy together because you're finally having sex with each other."

"That's just brilliant." Izzy let out a sigh.

"Ah, by the way, Andrew called last night."

She spun to face Shelly. "What for?"

"I didn't answer your phone. Didn't feel like being the person who had to tell him you'd already found a new guy and were still with him at three in the morning."

"He called at three?"

"And at two and at midnight."

"What doesn't he understand about *taking a break?*" Izzy picked up her phone and retrieved her messages.

"Hi, Iz." Andrew's voice sounded tinny in the phone speaker. "It's Thursday. Almost midnight. Just wanted to say sweet dreams. Give me a call when you get in."

That wasn't so bad.

The next message began to play. "Hey, Izzy. Where are you?" Andrew said. "I just wanted to talk. It's late…like two o'clock, so… You two are probably having a girls' night out. And, hey, you deserve it, you've been working hard. Be careful about guys in bars when it gets late. They only want one thing. Give me a call. Miss you."

Izzy fluffed her hair with one hand to help it dry and frowned at Shelly when the next message kicked in. "Okay, it's three-thirty in the morning and you're still not answering. I don't know what you're up to, maybe your phone is dead, but if I don't hear from you by the time I leave for work, I'm going to take the day off and head up there. I have a feeling you need me."

"Oh, no." Suddenly everything felt more out of control than ever. Izzy put the phone on Speaker and replayed the last message.

"Ack!" Shelly screeched as the voice mail shut off. "He's probably on his way already! That's all we need, your ex-boyfriend letting everyone know you're Elizabeth Gordon!"

Izzy quickly dialed Andrew's cell phone number. He barely got out hello before she said, "Andrew, everything is fine. There's no reason for you to come here."

"I was getting worried."

"There's no reason for you to come here," she repeated. She stepped restlessly across the living room, feeling caged by the continued rain and the topic of conversation.

"I didn't actually intend to. I have to be on the air today. Sweetheart, why didn't you call me back last night?"

Sweetheart? She exhaled slowly. "I was asleep. Shelly and I had a couple of drinks and I was exhausted—"

"Izzy, Izzy," he said patronizingly.

Her face grew hot and she wanted to scream. "Andrew, we broke up. We're over. We're—"

"Having a little rough spell?" he filled in helpfully. "Every relationship goes through things like this. Speed bumps, I like to call them."

Breakups was what she liked to call them. Still, much as she wanted to be brutally blunt, she couldn't do it. "I know you don't want to hear this," she said firmly, "but I meant what I said three nights ago. This isn't working. I think it's best if we go our separate ways. Please, Andrew, don't call me again."

"HI, GIB, WHAT'S ON YOUR MIND?" Bill Campbell rolled his chair away from the computer on his credenza and faced Gib. "Something change with the land sale?"

"Maybe. I had an interesting visitor the day before yesterday. Made me an offer. I'm not sure what to make of it—haven't even told my grandparents yet." He dug Jack Taylor's business card from his back pocket and held it out. "Ever hear of him?"

Bill took the card, examined the front and glanced at the unprinted back. "No, but that doesn't mean anything. Especially if he's not from around here. What did he want?"

"I'll lay it out." Gib grabbed a pad of paper from Bill's desktop and drew a quick map of the resort as he recapped Taylor's proposal about becoming partners. "Under this agreement, he'd own everything—even our buildings. I'm thinking we should counter. What if we propose that, once he owns the land, he has to sell us the acreage the resort sits on, including a piece of lake frontage?" He circled the areas on the map that he was talking about. "If my grandparents only needed enough money for that small amount of land, would they qualify for a loan then?"

"How many acres are we talking about?" Bill studied Gib's drawing.

"Maybe a third of the property."

"You think Taylor will go for it?"

Gib shrugged. "What choice does he have? Without us, he can't get any of the land."

Bill drummed his fingers on the armrest of his chair. "Considering everything, the smaller loan would be much more attractive to the bank. That is, assuming you're moving forward on those other changes we discussed."

"We're on it. Almost done with the first cottage— finished painting the last bedroom at two this morning." In his mind he saw Izzy refusing to leave him alone last night. She'd known better than he what was best for him. "Web site and brochure are in the works."

"That's encouraging," Bill said. "I can't promise anything, but if a smaller loan is the way you and the family want to go, we may be able to work something out."

LATER THAT AFTERNOON, Gib gathered his family in the screened porch off the second-floor living quarters at the lodge. The storm had passed hours ago and the day was now clear and sunny. Memories of childhood washed through him, the many summer evenings he spent relaxing out here when the work was finished. Surrounded by trees, a view of the lake in the distance, it was easy to feel like you were living high in the branches like a wild bird.

His grandparents were sitting in side-by-side brightly painted wood rockers. He watched them a moment and wondered what their reaction would be to this latest round of developments.

Matt charged through the door. "What's up?"

"I met with the bank this morning."

His brother threw him a look that clearly said, Didn't you hear me about going to Montana?

Matt sat on a wicker chair. "I told the Nelson kids I'd take them on a boat ride, so I don't have a lot of time."

"This won't take long. Some things have happened and I need to get everyone up to speed." Gib quickly detailed both the proposition he'd gotten from Jack Taylor and the counterproposal he wanted to make.

His grandfather stopped rocking and leaned forward. "You don't think we can get a loan for the whole place, is that it?"

"Put it this way. You have a lot better chance of getting a loan for a third of the land than you do for the whole thing." He sat on the wicker love seat and clasped his hands together. "Partnering with Taylor may be the only way we'll be able to stay here."

His grandfather's shoulders drooped and his brow furrowed. "What do you think, Matt? Sooner or later this place is going to be yours."

Matt's face froze. "Well— I—" He glanced at Gib, as though asking permission to tell all.

"Go ahead," Gib said. "Let's get everything on the table."

His grandmother rocked her chair harder, as if she knew something big was coming.

"I'm going to Montana this winter." Matt raised his eyes defiantly. "I'm not going to run the resort."

"Not this winter, you mean," Pete said.

"Not ever."

Catherine abruptly stopped her chair. "Matt?"

"I've got a job lined up. I've wanted to go for a long time."

"You talked to us about this way back in high school," she said. "I thought it was a daydream, not anything real."

Matt set his chin. "It's what I want to do. Ski patrol and work on the mountains."

"You knew about this?" His grandfather scowled at Gib.

"Only for a couple of days. The question is, now that you know Matt won't be here, what do you think about this partnership proposal?"

No one moved. It seemed as though minutes passed while he waited for an answer. A trio of birds chased past the screen. From down in the yard, Rascal let out a halfhearted bark, probably warning away a squirrel that had ventured too close. Finally his grandfather asked, "What do you think, Catherine?"

She looked from face to face. "I think… I want to go to Arizona."

Pete let out a too-loud guffaw. "I'm darn ready for a vacation, too. But what do you think about this proposal?"

"I don't mean a vacation. I mean, I want to move to Arizona. Matt doesn't want this place and neither do I. I'm tired. Forty years is a long time. I want to retire." Her words came slow, but strong. "Gib, I think you should tell that Taylor fella that we're not interested in a partnership—we want to sell the buildings. If he buys our buildings, he'll become the resort owner. And have right of first refusal to buy the land. Then we can get some money out of this place so we can get out."

"You want out?" Pete stared at his wife. "When did this happen?"

"It's been happening for a long time," she said. "I want to get up in the morning and not think about needing to make breakfast for fifty. I want to go to bed on a Friday night and not think about all those sheets that need to be washed the next day." She pushed the fingers of both hands through her hair and gazed up at the ceiling. "I know, I get to do that all winter. But it's been a long time since I got up on a summer morning and had coffee on the porch, read the paper, maybe even took a walk." She stood and faced her husband. "I love this piece of land, I love the resort, and I love you. But I think this is the end of the road."

"You're sure?"

"I'm tired, Pete. It's time." She went into the house.

His grandfather dropped his head into one hand for a few seconds. Then he sat back in his chair. "I'm sorry, Gib, for the mess we've put you through, but it sounds to me like you have your answer. Let's see what kind of money you can get from that developer. Maybe it'll give us something for our retirement." He followed his wife out of the room.

Gib leaned forward and rested his elbows on his knees. He turned to Matt, stunned. "You mean no one wants the resort? Then why the hell have I been working so hard?"

LATE THE NEXT MORNING, Izzy went into the bathroom and jiggled the handle on the toilet for the fifth time in twenty minutes. "Well, this could be a problem. The toilet keeps flushing itself and won't stop running."

Shelly looked up from the kitchen table where she was reviewing the previous day's footage on the laptop. "Why don't you call our resident handyman, Gib Murphy? Tell him to wear a tight white T-shirt and some snug-fitting jeans. And that you'll hand him his tools as he needs them."

"Don't be silly. We don't need to call Gib." She was about to take the chair next to Shelly when the phantom flusher struck again.

"You're right," Shelly said. "I think we need to listen to that toilet flush all day and night." She picked up the land line and dialed the main lodge. "If you don't want to hand Gib his tools, don't worry, I'll be able to find some time to help him out."

"It'll probably be Matt. Or Pete."

Shelly hung up the phone. "Catherine said someone would be out right away. Want to place a friendly wager on who?" She opened her purse. "Say, a five-spot? My money's on Gib."

"This project is really having an effect on you, isn't it?" Izzy pulled a five dollar bill from her wallet and laid it beside the one Shelly set on the table.

"I am so about to make five bucks," Shelly said. "Beautiful Boy is not going to pass up the opportunity to see you."

Izzy felt a tremor of excitement at the possibility Shelly could be right. "For the first time in my life, I'm actually hoping to lose."

Twenty minutes later, the sound of a vehicle driving up to the cottage sent them both racing to the door. As

Gib climbed out of the golf cart and took a toolbox from the backseat, Izzy felt a rush of nervous excitement.

"Is this the welcoming committee?" he asked, looking from one to the other.

Izzy knew she and Shelly were both grinning inanely.

"Just anxious for you to get here." Shelly strolled back into the living room.

"That was quick," Izzy said. From the corner of her eye, she saw her friend pick up the fives from the table and give each one a kiss. She'd probably never hear the end of this.

"We aim to please."

She followed Gib to the bathroom and leaned against the doorway as he pulled the top off the old tank and peered inside. "Probably needs a new flush valve," he said. "I've got a replacement unit in the cart."

Ten minutes later he had the whole thing taken apart, and much as Izzy told herself to go back to the computer, she couldn't tear herself away from watching him—the muscles in his arms, the way his shirt hung over the top of his shorts, the way his shorts fit his tight butt, the way his legs— He glanced up and caught her staring and she stammered out some nonsense like, "So that's all you do to fix it, huh?"

"Not rocket science, but it sure was a smart invention," he said, as though he couldn't believe they were actually having a conversation about toilet parts.

That made two of them.

"Now that you've got Hickory Hollow almost renovated, what hoop is next?" she asked in an effort to force her mind off him.

He finished what he was doing, then set the lid on

the tank and picked up his tool bag. "I think we're about done jumping."

"You got the loan?" She felt a surge of joy.

He shook his head and her emotions plummeted. She followed him to the door, fighting hard to hold back her concern. "What happened?"

He grabbed her with his free arm and pulled her close enough to plant a kiss on her forehead. "Nothing you need to worry your beautiful head about, Izzy. It's okay. Thanks for everything."

Before she could even react, he was out the door and climbing into the golf cart. "Happy flushing, ladies," he called.

She stared out the screen after him, surprised by his kiss and even more by his words. "Did you hear that?" she asked Shelly.

"*Happy flushing.* Nice. I liked the kiss more. And the extra five bucks wasn't bad, either," Shelly said.

"Not that. The thing about being done jumping. Something's wrong." She pulled open the door.

"Where are you going? We're supposed to be shooting at Ma Bailey's brothel in an hour."

"I'll be back in time. I have to know if the Murphys are losing the resort."

"And if they are? Then what?"

Izzy began to run down the road toward the main lodge. Then what? She had no clue.

AFTER PUTTING AWAY THE TOOLS, Gib cut into the woods, following the trail that had been worn through the brush by years of guests seeking solace in nature. He hoped he would be as fortunate today.

He veered away from the steps that had been cut into the steep hillside and reinforced with railroad ties. Ten minutes later, after hiking up an incline and cutting across a ridge, he broke out of the woods onto a hill overlooking the lake. His dad had showed him this place when he was a kid; he'd escaped here many times since then, mostly to find peace. This was where he'd come when he learned his parents died, when he'd gotten dumped by his first girlfriend, when he made the decision to leave White Bear to become a freelance photographer. It seemed only right that he came here now, when he was faced with selling off the resort. In a few hours, he would be meeting with Jack Taylor again, this time to propose a whole other arrangement—and if Jack agreed, the hourglass would begin to run out on White Bear Lodge.

He sat on the ground, forearms resting across his bent knees, and gazed down at the lake. Hard to believe in a few months this wouldn't belong to them anymore. He rolled onto his back and watched the white clouds wisp through the summer-blue sky, memories spilling over him like drops, softly at first, then harder and harder until, like driving rain, pain came with each remembrance. He closed his eyes a moment, then abruptly sat up. Maybe letting the resort go would be for the best. Maybe letting go of the past—all of it, childhood, young adulthood, Iraq—would let him sleep again at night.

There was no reason to put it off. It was his grandparents' wish, it was Matt's wish, and it was his wish, too.

A branch cracked behind him and he twisted 'round to see Izzy not fifteen feet away.

CHAPTER TWELVE

"HI." IZZY LOOKED DOWN AT her feet, suddenly feeling like she was trespassing. "I came up to the lodge to talk to you. Saw you cut into the woods…" She made a weak gesture with one hand and let it drop to her side, embarrassed to admit she'd followed him even though he had to know that was exactly what she'd done. She took a step forward. "What a gorgeous view."

"Menkesoq Lake."

"What does it mean?"

"Blueberry Moon. The Indians called the August moon blueberry moon, because that's when the blueberries ripen. Legend has it that an Indian princess met her true love during the blueberry moon and christened the lake such, so their love would be eternal." He put a hand on the ground next to him. "Have a seat."

She sat beside him cross-legged. "When you left the cottage, I got the feeling something had gone wrong with your plans… Has it?"

A pained expression flitted across his face. "Yes. And no."

She frowned, confused.

"Turns out, my brother is leaving for Montana in a couple months. Has a job lined up in Big Sky. He has no interest in running the resort. And my grandmother, well, she's right there with him."

"Moving to Big Sky?"

He pictured his grandma whipping down the mountains on skis. "Not hardly. She just wants out. Sick of changing sheets, making meals, the whole shooting match. When she heard Matt was leaving, she couldn't say she wanted to quit fast enough."

"Quit? You mean let the resort go? *No one wants to stay?*"

At his nod, relief rushed through her. They wouldn't lose the place they loved because of her family. This was their choice. The land could be sold. She and Shelly could make the documentary. Gib could go back to the other side of the world.

She felt a fleeting ache in her chest at that last thought.

"Funny thing is, I'm the only one who seems to be struggling with it," he said. "I'm meeting with a developer in a couple of hours to see if he wants to buy the resort from us, and it feels like I'm going to a wake."

"You'll always have the memories even if you don't own the resort."

"Yeah, I know." He rubbed a hand absently over the scar on his knee.

"This place doesn't define you or your family, Gib. It's just where you hung your hats awhile."

"Yeah, like a hundred years."

"Okay, a long while."

"I feel like I didn't do enough."

"You've only been home a few days. You're expecting too much of yourself." She pulled at the grass in front of her.

"Maybe I shouldn't have left in the first place. Or I should have come home more often and paid attention when I was here so I would have known how much they were struggling the past few years. I just feel like I could have done more." His voice was so low she had to strain to hear him.

Somehow she knew he wasn't just talking about the resort. "You gave everything you could at the time. I've been thinking about this on and off since you brought it up the other night. What the meaning, the purpose of life is." She put her hand on his. "And I realized it's this—*you do the best you can.* If at a given moment, you can only give eighty percent, then that's the best you can do. If it's fifty percent, then it's that. You can't look back later with the benefit of hindsight and say, *I could have done better.* You did the best you could at the time. That's what life is all about, Gib, doing the best you can."

He faced her, his emotions raw on his face, and she leaned forward to press her mouth to his as if to say it was time to replace bad memories with new ones. He kissed her back hard, the sort of kiss that begins with an almost desperate need to connect—intense, mouth open, tongues meshing, as if the contact could dull the pain. The day blurred and their surroundings disappeared, and it felt like the only things that were real were the two of them. Gib pulled back to look at her, and she felt the world begin to focus and she didn't want it to. She let herself sink into his gray eyes, his lashes so dark they were like a storm sweeping the sky.

His gaze was riveted on her face. She reached out to trace his lips with her fingers, and it was then she knew she wasn't doing this only for him, she was doing this for herself, as well.

"Izzy," he said, and the way his voice caressed each letter made a hot shiver skitter down her spine. Her body tightened from wanting him.

He bent to kiss her again, lightly touching one corner of her mouth and then the other, the line of her jaw, her throat, her lips. He drew her closer and she could feel the strength in his hands, and the tenderness. She sighed, loving the warmth of his mouth on hers, the heat of his body beside her. His fingertips traced the curve of her breast, slipped over her belly, and she felt every inch of her body constrict and soften at once.

"God, Izzy, stop me now or don't stop me," he murmured.

"No." She pulled him closer. "No stopping. No regrets."

His face was inches from hers, his eyes narrowed, the gray now almost invisible behind his lashes. He ran a thumb along her jaw and lips and followed it with his mouth. The heat from his touch skidded through her to settle in her core. Then he slid his hands up her back under her tank top, unclasped her bra and drew everything over her head. His T-shirt was soft against her skin, just a thin layer between them, but now even that was too much. She reached for the hem of his shirt and he raised his arms to let her pull it off. Then he pressed her down and onto her back in the soft, warm grass, the hair on his chest coarse against her breasts. He popped the button at the top of her capris and pulled down the zipper. "I want to see you naked in the sunlight," he murmured, and tugged them off her, his fingers touching her, making her wonderfully crazy.

"Ditto." She reached for the buckle of his belt and pulled it open.

"Ditto?" he said as he lifted his hips to let her strip off his shorts. A cloud passed in front of the sun, darkening the day and his face for a moment, making him appear dangerous and mysterious and sexy all at once. He kissed her breast, teased her with his tongue until she shuddered with wanting him. She skimmed her hands along his hips, up the muscles of his arms as she pulled him toward her, so she could taste the heat of his mouth again.

"You're something else," he murmured, his breath tickling her cheek. "My blueberry moon princess." He cupped her face with his hands and kissed her until she was dizzy.

She loved how his hard body felt pressed to hers, loved the feel of his calloused fingers on her soft skin, loved the heat between them. He slid a hand lower and she closed her eyes and gave herself up to the moment, to the pressure building inside her. He stroked her until she was nearly out of her mind, her blood thickening, every nerve screaming. He rolled onto her, and she arched up to meet him, reveling in the feel of him, his lips, the weight of him pressing her back, the rest of the world gone missing. His hands were holding her head, fingers twined in her hair. "Come on, Izzy," he breathed into her ear. The tickle of his breath was the last thing she could handle, and she broke with him, like the sun shattering into a million little pieces. She gasped at how right he felt, how she could feel him in every cell of her body as though he should have been there all along and she'd only just realized he'd been missing.

She kept her eyes closed, basking in her joy, feeling more free than she ever had in her life.

"Izzy."

She cracked her eyes open.

"You're incredible," he said, awe tingeing his voice.

"*We* were incredible."

"Yeah." He rolled onto his side and wrapped her in his arms, and she let herself relax against him, content. She could smell wildflowers and leaves and blossoms on the breeze and the smell of the two of them mingled with all of that and she took it in, let it fill her. She thought to herself that it had never been like this with Andrew, and marveled that, in the past few weeks, everything had gotten sharper, as if her life had been a movie out of focus and someone had finally showed her how to get rid of the fuzzy edges.

Gib nibbled at her ear. "I never guessed there was such a wild woman inside you."

Neither had she. *No regrets,* she'd said. And she had none. Not where Gib was concerned. This was just another step along her path to taking back her own life and following her dreams. She thought of how she would leave here in a week—and *never see Gib again.* A tiny doubt tried to rise in her and she shoved it down. She'd made her decision and there was no room for second-guessing.

Gib ran a hand down her arm, fingers touching the sensitive skin on the inside of her elbow. Her breath caught. He put his lips to the spot and tickled it with his tongue. She shivered and curled toward him, relishing the nearness of him, not wanting to let him go.

He chuckled softly. "Honey, you are awfully tempting. Too bad I scheduled that meeting because I'd much rather stay here with you."

"Ohmigosh, what time is it?" She sat up and scrambled for her clothes. "Shelly and I are supposed to be in Minocqua to do an interview at a brothel from the thirties." She brushed the grass off her clothes and ran her fingers through her hair. "How do I look?"

"Like a million bucks." Gib pulled on his shorts and T-shirt.

"Thanks for that lie. Now, how do we get out of here?"

As he led the way into the brush, she admired his strong legs and his broad shoulders, the way he moved through the uneven terrain so easily. He reached for her hand and she took it, not quite ready to let go of him, her heart still warm and full with what they'd shared. This had been one of the most wonderful, spontaneous times in her entire life. Just she and Gib. *And the resort and the land and Elizabeth Gordon and the documentary and his memories of Iraq and—*

In the distance, thunder rumbled.

"Sounds like more rain coming," Gib said.

Didn't matter. All that mattered was that the Murphys didn't want the land. Her family could sell and she didn't have to worry about Gib's grandparents losing everything they'd ever had. She could make her documentary and move forward with her own life, without having to worry about leaving carnage in her wake.

THEY BROKE OUT OF THE WOODS near the main lodge, and Gib grabbed Izzy by the arm and pulled her round the back of the work shed to kiss her one more time. The sky had darkened ominously and a couple of rogue raindrops splashed onto them.

"Hey, I thought you had a meeting to get to," she said. "And I have a movie to make. And we're both going to get drenched if we're not careful."

"Who cares?"

She punched his shoulder playfully. "I do. If I'm late, I'll lose my interview. I hate to damage your male ego, but it's the most important thing to me right now."

He put a hand on his heart as though mortally wounded. "Go, then. Go and leave me to suffer here by the wayside."

She took a couple of half skips away and he thought to himself that for the first time in a long time, he'd caught a lucky break. More raindrops splashed down and he took the steps to the lodge veranda. "Good luck with the interview," he called after her.

She waved to him over her shoulder and he pictured her captured in the lens of his camera, her eyes dancing, the wind tossing her hair, her smile wide and happy, and a well-loved look of contentment on her face. He thought of how she'd been less than an hour ago, naked in the summer sun, loving him outside with abandon. The rain began to fall harder, and she dashed to the trail leading to her cottage, both hands on top of her head as though she could keep herself dry that way.

He stayed there, watching, long past the point when she disappeared into the trees. Overhead, lightning sliced open the dark clouds, releasing a torrent of water that poured from the sky in great silver panels and rolled in rivulets down the gravel drive and into the grass. It was cooler now and fresher, the cleansing rain washing away the dust clogging the air.

Like beautiful Izzy Stuart had done with his day. He didn't know where this was going, wasn't sure there was anywhere for it to go, but he knew, without a doubt, right now he wanted more of Izzy Stuart in his life.

JACK TAYLOR WAS SAYING something sympathetic about all the years the Murphy family had lived on the land at White Bear. His white shirt was perfectly starched, his collar open and his tie loosened around his neck like some *GQ* model.

He sat opposite Gib in a booth at a family restaurant two hours south of Menkesoq Lake, tapping his yellow legal pad with the tip of his pencil, then the eraser, then the tip again. As though he were in a hurry.

Not that he was a bad guy. Maybe for him, life was best lived in a rush. Finish up one job and on to the next. No time to waste. No time like the present to make a shitload of money. Wasn't Gib's cup of tea, but it took all kinds to make the world go round. He'd sure been in a hurry to meet again once Gib called him about the family's decision.

"I like it. I become the sole owner of White Bear Lodge. Then I assume the existing lease and have first rights to match any offer the landowners get." Jack nodded appreciatively. "I really like it."

"My grandparents haven't said anything about wanting to retire," Gib lied, not wanting Taylor to think the family was so desperate to get out they'd accept a lowball offer for the resort. "They don't even know I'm proposing this. But they're getting to that age, and if they got an acceptable offer for the buildings, my brother and I think they might see things differently."

"I'm sure we can come to an agreement," Jack said. "I'll have to have the place appraised—quickly. The cottages are all pretty old, aren't they?"

The waitress arrived with their order—two cups of coffee and a plate of cherry Danish kringle—and put everything dead center on the table, including their check.

Gib sipped his coffee and frowned at the taste, strong and bitter. "With all due respect, our buildings are worth a lot more than their appraised value. Because…without them, you can't get the land."

Jack scribbled some notes on the paper. "Absolutely. I know that. But a brick-and-mortar appraisal will give us a jumping-off point."

Better be a big jump.

"I know this must be for hard for you after all the years your family's been on the land," Jack said. "I was thinking on the way here, I'd throw in a week's vacation for your family every year at the condos, dinners included. I'm hoping to get approval for a rib-and-steak house overlooking the water. It'll draw customers from all around the area."

Gib gripped his coffee mug with both hands. One week. Lifetimes of his family's memories distilled down to one week. No more breakfasts on the veranda, lazy quiet days at the beach, no more hikes through the woods. He'd never show his own children the secret place at the top of the hill—for them, it would have to be just another story their father had to tell.

No. No one-week vacations here for him. When this was over, he didn't ever want to come back.

"Let me get back to my office, get an appraiser on the job and see what we can come up with." Jack took a bite of kringle. "I take it you're selling the place complete. All the canoes, kayaks, paddleboats, equipment, you name it?"

"I'm sure there's some furniture and other things my grandparents will want to take with them." Gib tried to shake off the feeling that he'd just learned of another death.

"That's fine. As far as what my company would keep…we much prefer to start with things new. If you want, you could have a big sale before we take ownership. Clear everything out before we clear the land." Jack took another bite of kringle.

"Clear the land?"

"Take down the buildings," he said once he swallowed his food.

Of course they'd raze the buildings. Why wouldn't they? Way more money to be made with rows of condos than with little cottages scattered in the woods.

"We may have to clear out some trees, too, but we won't know that until the architectural design is finished." Jack popped the last bite of kringle into his mouth and licked his fingers. "This is delicious. Famous Racine kringle," he said. "Have some."

Gib shook his head, unable to speak for the pictures in his head. He couldn't eat right now if his life depended on it. "I've got to get back," he finally said. "Still have resort guests expecting dinner even if we are planning to sell out soon."

"The work is never done, I imagine. When you tell your grandparents that I'd like to buy the buildings, tell them that peace, quiet and a rocking chair are right around the corner."

Gib slid out of the booth and shook Jack's hand. Peace, quiet and a rocking chair. They already had that. At one of the best places you could ever find.

AFTER FINISHING THE INTERVIEW at the former brothel, Izzy and Shelly drove an hour to Elcho to check out the rumor that the town had housed a medical way station for Prohibition-era mobsters escaping to and from Wisconsin. They caught dinner at a diner along the way and didn't get back to White Bear until early evening.

By then, the rain was long gone, the sky clear, the temperature comfortable. Izzy left Shelly reading in their cabin and walked briskly along the lakeside trail, past white birch trees and maples and evergreens. The smell of pine hung heavy in the air. Though she'd always loved the outdoors, she'd spent less and less time there the past few years. Lately, it had been Andrew's fault—air-conditioning and central heating were his favored climes. But she couldn't blame this all on him; somehow, even she always had something else to do.

She spotted Matt raking the sand, cleaning up pine needles, sticks and leaves that had blown onto the beach during the storm. He stopped working as she drew near. "How's the movie business?"

"Wonderful. There are so many gangster stories up here, we could stay a month." She gazed out onto the lake and saw Gib giving a kayak lesson. Warmth spread across her chest as she watched him, admired his confidence, his strength, remembered making love with him that afternoon.

"He's a man of many talents," Matt said.

She felt a blush race up her cheeks. He couldn't possibly know, could he? "What? Oh, I'm—"

"Whatever Gib decides to do, he does well. Used to drive me crazy when we were younger. I was always the tagalong trying to keep up with him." Matt leaned on his rake. "Until he took up photography. I couldn't have cared less about taking pictures."

"I hear you're a good skier."

He grinned proudly. "Gib was into photography and I was into going fast and adrenaline rushes."

"And now?" she asked.

"I'm still into going fast and adrenaline rushes." He focused on his brother again. "But Gib doesn't shoot pictures anymore."

"I thought he just got back from an overseas assignment."

"He did. But he hasn't taken a picture since he got home. Hasn't even taken his camera out of his room."

"Maybe he wants a break."

Matt bent to scoop up several broken sticks. "That camera used to be like another appendage for him. He was never without it. Now he's never with it."

She closed her eyes a moment. Gib's injuries went deeper than she'd even realized. "After everything he's been through, maybe all he needs is more time."

"I hope so." Matt used the rake to drag the pile of debris toward the treeline.

Izzy looked between the brothers. She wanted to say she would be here for Gib—

But would she?

For another week.

Much as she liked Gib, she had plans for her life.

With any luck, this documentary would lead to better things and bigger cities. Hopefully, Gib would be heading out again, too, to gift the world with his photos.

And if he couldn't?

The thought almost brought tears to her eyes.

THE SUN HAD GONE DOWN hours ago, but, even at eleven o'clock, its heat still lingered. Gib sat on the veranda alone, drinking a beer as he contemplated the events of the day. Though he tried to stay focused on his discussion with Jack Taylor, memories of making love with Izzy kept hijacking his mind. He wanted to be with her tonight, see her beautiful smile, her dancing eyes. He wanted to put his arms around her and feel her mouth beneath his.

Before she was gone.

Maybe he shouldn't get any more involved; she would be here only another week at the most. The thought made him vaguely restless, and he set the half-full bottle on the floor next to his chair and stood. Izzy would be here only another week. All the more reason to see her tonight.

Ten minutes later, he knocked on the door to her cottage, fully intending to ask how their shoot at the old brothel had gone today. But when Izzy pulled open the door wearing a little tank top and shorts, her hair tousled around her face and her eyes bedroom sleepy, he lost all coherent thought.

"Gib? Is something the matter?" She cast a glance at her watch.

He snapped his brain back into working order. "No, no, everything's fine. Did I wake you?"

She wrinkled her nose as she squeezed her eyes shut then opened them again. "I dozed off in the chair watching the news. Shelly's asleep on the couch. Long day."

"Yeah, me too." Suddenly he felt awkward and stupid for showing up at her door this late.

"You want to come in?"

"No. I don't want to wake Shelly up."

She squinted at him. He could tell by her expression she was trying to figure out what he was doing here.

"How'd your meeting go this afternoon?" she finally asked.

"Not bad. I'm waiting to hear back from him."

After a pause, she said, "Okay, so, um, you came by to say *hi?*" The corners of her lips twitched.

No, he didn't just want to say hi. He took her hand and tugged her out into the darkness of the stoop, closing the door behind them. "Actually, I wanted to kiss you good-night."

Her mouth curved into a shy smile as he pulled her close and bent to touch her lips with his. She slipped her arms up his chest and around his neck, leaned into him, and he kissed her harder, experiencing a rush of emotion so fast and strong he actually felt weak. He pressed her back against the building for support, and their movement knocked the hanging metal bell to the ground with a crash and a clang. The sound jarred them apart.

The front door whipped open and Shelly stood in the doorway, hair sticking out every which way, eyes narrowed. "Was that you two?" she demanded before slamming the door shut.

He and Izzy began to laugh.

"Guess I'd better get going," he said.

"Thanks for stopping."

He started down the road toward the lodge, all his thoughts focused on Izzy. Everything about her, *everything,* was right.

Too bad every other circumstance was wrong.

CHAPTER THIRTEEN

THE CALL FROM JACK TAYLOR came in at eleven the next morning. Gib recognized the number on his cell and stepped out of the lodge for privacy.

Taylor wasted no time getting right to the point. "I talked to my partner about your question, Gib, and we're in agreement. We'd be happy to buy the resort. Our appraiser examined fair market values and we went from there. Building in, of course, compensation for the intangible benefit we'll receive as the owner. I can fax our offer or e-mail it. Which would you prefer?"

Though this was exactly the response he expected, Gib still felt a jolt at the news. The resort was gone. In a few short weeks—months at most—this wouldn't be home anymore. He thought he'd come to grips with it yesterday when he was with Izzy, but apparently not.

How could Matt not want to stay here?

"Gib? Did I lose you?"

"No, no, I'm here."

"You want a fax or e-mail?"

No fax. He didn't want anyone else to see the offer yet; it made everything too real. He wanted some time to think about it without three other cooks in the kitchen. "E-mail would be fine." He flatly recited his e-mail address. "Once I print a hard copy, I'll get the family together—have to see when everyone's available—and we'll talk it over."

"Super. I'll wait to hear from you."

Gib closed his phone. "You do that," he muttered, feeling animosity toward Jack Taylor and not sure why. The guy sounded like he would be pretty damn fair with his offer. Besides, he was making it possible for the family to leave White Bear with something in the bank instead of going away broke.

Couldn't ask for more than that, could you?

A freshening breeze kissed his cheek, and Gib raised his head to stare out at the lake where whitecaps were skipping across the water and a sailboat heeled in the wind. Above him, the leaves in the trees fluttered and spun dark and light green like costumed dancers in the sunlight. He shaded his eyes with one hand and watched the children leaping from the float and screaming as they hit the cool water, their parents reclining on lounge chairs in the sun, all cares left behind.

Regret skidded through him. White Bear had given so many people memories that would last a lifetime. It had given him and Matt a home when his parents died. A good home. A happy home even though it had changed from being a fun summer vacationland to work camp all in the blink of an eye. Years of doting on guests, serving meals, changing bedding, mowing lawns, hiking, sailing, campfires, gold and red trees in autumn, the leaves spinning to the ground with every fall breeze, snowdrifts reaching up into the lower tree branches, cross-country skiing through the woods and coming back to a fire in the hearth—

He'd hated it here.

Hadn't he?

It was too late for melancholy visits down memory lane. Everyone wanted out, him included. White Bear Lodge was about to be no more. All he had to do was retrieve the offer from his e-mail and get the family's approval. Contracts would be drawn, signatures affixed, and it would be finished.

The Gordon family would get the money they wanted. Jack Taylor would get the land he wanted. Grandma and Grandpa would get the retirement they wanted. Matt would get the freedom he wanted. And him, he would get…what was it he wanted?

As though holding a camera, he raised his hands to frame the beach scene in a rectangle formed by his thumbs and index fingers. Then he turned and shot an imaginary picture of the tall pines on the edge of the forest, and yet another of the only log cottage visible from where he was standing.

What he wanted was picture-perfect serenity.

And that was here.

Nah, couldn't be. He couldn't be thinking he wanted to stay here. He'd gone halfway around the world to discover the place he wanted was here?

His grandfather came up the hill and gave him a strange look. "What are you doing?"

"Taking pictures so I don't forget what it looks like."

"There's a lot of memories out there. Yours. Mine. Your father's. My father's. His father's. It's in the trees, the sand, the grass, the water."

"Our family is this place," Gib said quietly. "Our DNA is probably all over it. I can't believe I'm having trouble letting go."

The older man put an arm around Gib's shoulders. "To all things a season. Don't beat yourself up. We've had a hundred good years here. That's a lot more than most families get anywhere. Time has a way of moving on whether we want it to or not."

Matt stuck his head out of the side door of the lodge. "Hey, Gramps, Grandma said to hurry up," he called.

"Still have plenty of chores to do even if we are going to sell," his grandfather said.

Sell. Somehow it felt less like they were selling and more like they were selling out.

As their grandfather went into the lodge, Matt came out. "You heard back from that developer yet?"

"Nope," Gib lied.

"Wish he'd hurry up and put us out of our misery."

"For some reason, I'm not feeling the misery anymore."

"That's because you've been gone so long. Me? I can smell liberty already. I feel like the chains that bind me are loosening."

Gib opened his arms wide. "Be strange not to call this place home, don't you think?"

"Yeah. But I'll get over it."

"That's an awfully cavalier attitude." Why was he looking to his brother for validation? The kid was too young to realize what he was losing.

"No, it's not. I've had plenty of years here to think about what I want. And what I want is to be free."

"Regular jobs tie you down, too." An idea rooted in his mind and he took several steps in either direction as he surveyed the land, the lake and the main lodge.

"Not like a resort does." Matt went up the stairs and opened the door. "You coming inside?"

Gib shook his head and watched the screen door swing shut behind his brother. "Not yet. There's something I have to check out." He set off down the path that led to Izzy's cabin.

AFTER HALF A DAY SPENT filming at two other locations reputed to be gangster-vacation hideaways, Izzy wanted nothing more than to lie in her chaise longue in the late afternoon sun. She couldn't stop thinking about making love with Gib yesterday afternoon, about how he'd come to the cabin to kiss her good-night.

Shelly was stretched out on the adjacent lounge chair, *Cosmo* magazine open on her lap. "Can you believe we've been here seven days already? We've accomplished almost everything we wanted to do." She perused the checklist they had started the first day at White Bear, a list that had expanded quite a bit in the past week. "Interview the grandfather," she read aloud. "Follow up on other alleged stories and locations. Track down family members of former resort owners who may have stories to tell. Dump Andrew."

"That's on the list?"

"It was always on my version of the list." Shelly tapped a finger against her lower lip. "Let's see, what else? Meet some handsome guys at the resort."

Izzy sat up straight and grabbed for the notepad. Shelly held it away from her, then brought it close enough to read aloud again. "Interview owners of a former brothel. Investigate Murphy family's current organized crime connections."

"Of which, if there are connections, we don't want

to know, so that we don't end up in a block of concrete," Izzy said.

"Agreed. I'm not up for taking on the mob." Shelly ran a finger down the sheet. "Screen music. Begin to edit on the computer. Oh, and have a vacation relationship with Gib Murphy. Yes, I think all our plans are coming to fruition nicely."

"It's not a *relationship*. You didn't actually write that down, did you?" Izzy tried, again unsuccessfully, to snatch the pad.

"What's wrong with having a relationship with Beautiful Boy? You sure didn't have a problem having one with *Andrew*. Anyway, you haven't given me many details about what's going on, so how would I know?"

"Shelly."

"Yes? Did you have something you wanted to share with me?"

Izzy huffed and dropped back against her chaise longue. "Well, he can kiss, believe me—"

"And?"

"*That,* too." *Oh, yeah, that, too.* "But he's got so much stuff on his mind and in his life. And I do, too. After two stifling years with Andrew—"

"Funny, you never called it 'stifling' before."

Izzy felt her eyes widen in amazement. "I never thought of it that way before."

"Leaps and bounds forward. Nice to see." Shelly flipped another page in the magazine.

"Anyway, I've only just gotten my freedom and I like it."

"Methinks the lady doth protest too much."

"No, really. I like being able to decide what *I* want

to do each day. It got old always deferring to Andrew on things."

"Somehow, I can't picture Gib ever telling you not to wear flip-flops in public because the flipping noise is *classless.*"

Izzy frowned at the memory of that conversation with Andrew. It had come on the heels of another discussion about wearing beaters, the tank tops modeled after men's sleeveless undershirts. "Well, the point is, I just got rid of Andrew. I don't need to tie myself down with someone else right away—especially now when I'm going after a new career."

"Girlfriend, you've been getting rid of Andrew for months. You just didn't realize it. That's why you're not having any second thoughts." She paused. "You're not…are you?"

"No." Realization smacked Izzy hard. Shelly was right. Her relationship with Andrew had been over a long time ago, but she'd refused to see it. Because everyone thought Andrew was *perfect.* She could almost cry. Thank goodness, she'd found her way out of that.

"'Ten Things He'll Never Tell You But Wishes You Knew,'" Shelly read aloud.

"What?"

"Headline story. Hmm. These are interesting. I never knew you could do *that* with a shoestring…."

Izzy opened her book. She heard Shelly turn several pages.

"Not to mention 'Hot Tips to Make Your Nights Sizzle.' Any interest in hearing more?"

Izzy ignored her.

"Because you know, sizzling nights are always nice to have. Sure beats nonsizzling nights. Of course, here at White Bear Lodge, some of the guests have sizzling days *and* nights, while others of us are left searching for any lukewarm attention we can get."

"Lalalalala," Izzy sang, sticking her fingers in her ears. "I can't hear you."

"Hey, I'm not the person who bought this magazine in the minimart—"

"It had an interview with Matt Damon—"

"And a few other articles, as well. How about 'Techniques to Make Him Putty in Your Hands.' Hmm, I wonder what parts will be like putty. It would seem that the goal wouldn't be to have your man like *putty* but rather—"

"Stop!" Izzy sat up. "He needed me at that moment. And, maybe I needed him, too. *At that moment.* But nothing can—or should—go on between us. I'm building a new life and it can't involve being tied down." Though she was saying all the right words, none of them felt true. She threw her arms skyward as if to toss away her doubts. "You and I are aiming for the stars with this documentary, and I intend for us to land in the Milky Way. Now, if you'll excuse me, I'm going to take a little nap here in the sun." *And daydream about making love with Gib.*

After a long pause, Shelly said, "Okay, I can take a hint. No one ever said I was totally dense. But I have to ask one more thing, because this truly is important. And then I won't bother you again."

Izzy didn't open her eyes. "Promise?"

"Promise."

"What's the question?" She heard the sound of pages flipping.

"So, what about 'Sexy Moves to Spice up Your Love Life'? You do want to keep Gib happy, don't you?"

Izzy glared at her friend.

"Hello, ladies." Gib's voice came from somewhere not very far behind them.

Izzy bolted upright, heart pounding into overdrive. God help her—God help Shelly—if he'd overheard any of this conversation. "The list! Where's that list?" she hissed. "Get that thing hidden." She turned quickly and almost gasped at the sight of Gib, more Beautiful Boy than ever, a stripe of sunburn across his nose underlining those luscious gray-blue eyes. He shoved his hands into the pockets of his baggy shorts and she remembered how those hands had made her shiver yesterday. She didn't think she could speak more than one word without her voice trembling. "Hi."

Shelly swung her legs over the side of her chair and, in one fluid movement, scooped up the magazine, the notepad and her towel. She sashayed toward the cottage door. "Hello, Gib. Go ahead and take my chair. Time for this bathing beauty to take a break. I think I'm getting sunburned."

As the cottage door banged shut behind her, Gib sat on the edge of the longue. "Sunburned? She's fully dressed. And it's four o'clock."

Izzy cast a sideways glance at his muscular legs, visions of yesterday crowding her mind again. "She burns easily—pale skin, you know." She met his eyes and felt her stomach flop. This was ridiculous. She couldn't like him. He had too much baggage and she was a free woman with no ties. *Free.*

"Filming going okay?" He clasped his hands

together, strong hands that had made her shiver with joy yesterday. *What had Shelly been saying about a shoe-string?* For goodness' sake, she knew better than to go down this path. "Uh, we got some great footage today in Woodruff." She blathered on nervously. "At the Plantation Supper Club—used to be a fancy nightclub casino in the twenties. Then we stopped by the library and found a bunch of old newspaper stories. And called the museum for old letters people may have donated." She clenched her teeth together to stop her rambling. "How about you? Have you heard anything from that developer you met with?"

"He called this morning to make an offer."

"That's wonderful."

"Maybe." He sat back into the chair and put his feet up. "Something doesn't feel right."

"You don't trust him?"

"He's okay. His vision for developing the land doesn't mirror anything I would do, but, no, I think he's on the up and up, if that's what you're asking." There was a troubled undertone in his voice.

"It sounds like the perfect solution. What do the others think?"

"I haven't told anyone yet. It's like…if nobody knows about the offer, it can't happen." He rubbed his eyes.

"Yeah. White Bear has been in your family a long time," she said.

He shrugged. "I wish this wasn't all happening under the gun. That I had more time to think it over."

Think what over? His grandparents and brother had made their decisions; they didn't want to stay.

"Look around here." He gestured at the woods. "When I compare this to places I've been, it's hard not to see it as a piece of heaven. I know this sounds crazy— I mean, who in their right mind would want to take on a struggling resort? But every time I think about giving it to someone else…"

He couldn't possibly be changing his mind about staying here…could he? It had been such a relief to know his family was *choosing* to leave White Bear Lodge, that her parents wouldn't be throwing them out of their home. "What are you saying?" She held her breath.

"I'm thinking," he said slowly, "that I should try to make a go of it here. I have an idea…hardly more than a couple of thoughts right now. This would be an incredible place to hold retreats, training seminars, corporate team-building programs." Enthusiasm crept into his voice. "We have plenty of sleeping capacity. And the lodge can accommodate some pretty big groups. But…it'll never work if the woods are gone and we only own a small piece of land with limited beach access from the sprawling condo development next door. If I'm going to do this, I'd have to own all the land." He leaned toward her, his expression intense. "I need a completely unbiased opinion. Izzy, do you think it will work?"

She looked at him, stunned. How could she encourage him when she knew he probably wouldn't qualify for a loan to buy the land? "I don't know what to say. It isn't my opinion that matters so much—it's the bank's. That's who you need to ask," she said quietly. If he got turned down, this man who had lost so much already would lose even more. Her heart wrenched. "Gib, a few days ago you said you'd never stay here. You liked not knowing what the next day would bring. This is such a sudden change of heart."

"People change all the time."

Not usually overnight. "But what if your wanting to stay is only a response to what you went through in Iraq. And to your friend dying recently…and to you not taking pictures anymore."

His brow furrowed. "Who—"

"Matt. He only mentioned it once. Didn't say much. Gib, maybe you're just reacting—"

"But is that wrong? People change their lives, their direction, all the time because of something that happens to them. A circumstance sends them down a new path. Hasn't that ever happened to you?"

Yes. It was the reason she was here. A letter she'd written herself ten years ago had propelled her into making a movie, into taking charge of her life, into making love on a hillside with Gib on a summer afternoon. "Actually, it has," she said slowly.

"Then I value your opinion even more. What do you think, Izzy?"

Her heart slammed against her chest. "You can't ask me that. I don't have a crystal ball. I don't want to be responsible—" She stopped. No matter how she tried to spin it, she—her family—was responsible for him being in this position.

"So you really don't think it will work?"

"I'm worried that you want to stay because of all the bad things that have happened in the past few months. With everything you've been through, it's only natural to want to hang on to your past. It's security, a safety net. But what happens if you stay and in six months decide you've made a mistake?" She gazed into the branches overhead and hated that she had to say the words coming out of her mouth. "You asked what I think. Well, here it is. You should take some pictures again. If for no other reason than to make sure you aren't choosing something just because you're running from something else."

He didn't say anything for a long minute. "You think I'm running?"

She shrugged.

"Maybe you're right. I guess it's time to tell the others about the offer."

CHAPTER FOURTEEN

HE PUT OFF TELLING ANYONE until the next morning, until he'd had a chance to make lists, compare pros and cons, and determine whether his interest in staying was simply a reaction to what had happened to him in Iraq. After hours of analyzing himself from every angle, he finally listened to his gut and made a decision. He wanted to go for it.

He crossed the southwestern-design rug in the living room and positioned himself in front of the TV, blocking the Brewers-Cubs game that his grandparents and Matt were watching. From where he stood, he had a perfect view of the room, its American Indian framed paintings on the walls, its comfortably worn, over-stuffed furniture in terra-cotta and turquoise blue, its black wrought-iron table lamps. This was home. It had always been home. He wanted it to stay that way.

"You make a better door than a window." Matt lounged full length on the couch, a bottle of water in his hand. He took a drink. "Get out of the way."

Gib grinned but didn't move.

Matt lobbed a throw pillow at him and Gib knocked it out of the way. "I heard from the developer," Gib said. "You want to talk about it now or after the game?"

"Now," all three said simultaneously. Matt sat upright and clicked off the set.

"Thought so." Even though he'd carefully planned what to say, his stomach was still jumping nervously. "Jack Taylor called me yesterday. He's made an offer." Gib handed out printed copies of the e-mail he'd received. "Bottom line, he's willing to buy the resort from us, lock, stock and barrel. This spells out all the high points. If we agree in principle, he'll have an official offer drawn up."

Matt scanned the single sheet of paper. "Sweet."

Gib dragged a straight-backed chair away from the wall and sat down facing his family. He began to run through the financial terms, keeping everything matter-of-fact, as though simply ticking off the details of a business merger to which they had no personal connection. "He proposes that he buy the buildings immediately and we stay on to finish out the season as managers. Since it's already August, we're about done, anyway. We'll need to decide what we want to keep— furniture, you name it. We can sell everything else in an estate sale or he'll buy it as part of the package. He'd like to close within the week. That will give him the next week to get financing in place to match the offer the Gordons received for the land."

He looked into the faces of his grandparents and brother. "It'll also be the end of White Bear Lodge. Hard to believe after all these years."

His grandfather drooped as if the air had been sucked out of him, and his grandmother reached between their chairs to take his hand. "You gave it everything you had, honey," she said. "Forty years. The world is changing.

People don't want to go to places like this anymore. They all want to own cottages now."

Gib cleared his throat. "There's a little more."

"There's nothing else on the sheet," Matt said. "I don't like the sound of this."

"I've been doing a lot of thinking." Gib stood and crossed the room. "The more I think about letting this place go, the less I like the picture in my head."

"This doesn't sound good at all." Matt waved a hand back and forth. "Hey, Gib? No, this is not a—"

"Honey, let him finish," his grandmother said.

"I know what he's saying and it's not anything you want to hear. Gib, listen to me. Think long-term. Don't be an idiot," Matt said.

"Shut up," Gib said to his brother. "Just because you want to go to Montana doesn't mean I want to."

"This isn't about Montana—"

"Boys!" their grandmother said. "What is going on?"

"Gib's being stupid—"

"I hate the thought of someone else on this property. I want to take over the resort." Gib abruptly sat in the hard-backed chair again, like a kid waiting to find out if he was going to be punished.

Absolute silence met his pronouncement.

"Don't be expecting me to congratulate you," Matt finally muttered.

"Don't everyone jump for joy at once," Gib said.

His grandfather leaned forward, brows pulled together in a deep V. "Ten days ago you were dead set against being the manager. Now you want to stay on for the long haul? Don't get me wrong, Gib, I'd love you to stay. But feeling guilty about letting the resort go to someone else isn't a good enough reason to take this place on."

"It's not that."

"And it can't be because you're too afraid to pick up your camera anymore," Matt said pointedly.

His brother needed to learn when to keep his mouth shut. "I've been through a lot of stuff this past year. Lost people who were important to me. Coming home made me realize what else I could lose."

"You can't use this place to hide out from the rest of the world." Matt toyed with the remote control. "Have you shot one photograph since you got back?"

"What does that have to do with it?"

"You're running away." Matt slouched into the couch and aimed the controller at the TV but didn't press the on button. "White Bear Lodge is just a place to hide from your feelings."

"When the hell did you become a psychologist?" Gib snapped, irritated that both Izzy's and Matt's responses had been the same. He eyed his grandparents. "I thought you'd all be happy the resort wouldn't be leaving the family."

His grandfather pushed himself to standing. "We are. Gib, nothing would make me happier than to know one of you boys wanted to stay."

"We're just surprised. It's such a turnabout," his grandmother said.

"And stupid," Matt added. "Come the middle of winter, you're going to regret it and then you'll be stuck. You're making a rash decision because the land's about to be sold. In six months I don't want to hear about how—"

"Wait a darned minute." His grandfather held up a hand. "Are you thinking you'll accept that first proposal from Taylor? The one that gives him ownership but lets us stay on to run White Bear?"

Gib picked up the e-mail offer. "I don't think the resort would survive that agreement. There'd be development all around White Bear. We'd lose the best property and only have access to someone else's beach. The ambience would disappear and so would the privacy."

"You want to buy all the land?" Matt asked.

Gib nodded. "I know getting the loan is a longshot, but I have a plan for increasing business. If the bank likes it, maybe it will help." He looked down for a moment. "I want to position the resort as a place to hold training seminars and corporate team-building programs, even retreats. We've got the lodge, we've got sixteen cabins—two and three bedrooms apiece. That's accommodations for at least sixty-five. We've also got enough land to give people the space they need to find solitude…so they can find themselves."

"You're sounding kind of new age-y," Matt said. "You sure you didn't get a blow to the head recently? And where does this leave Grandma and Grampa as far as retirement?"

"Matthew!" Their grandmother brought her hands together with a clap. "If Gib wants to stay—"

"He makes a valid point." Gib walked to the window overlooking the front lawn. "Selling White Bear will give you the money you need to retire. If I take over, it means you're stuck here."

"Don't you worry about us. Your grandfather and I will be all right."

"If you want to stay, we'll do whatever we can to help you," Pete said.

Gib ran a hand through his hair. "I don't have everything figured out yet. I just wanted to let you know about the proposal. And get your reactions to what I've been thinking. Let me tell the bank my plan. Show them our progress renovating the first cottage, the Web site, the brochure. See if I even have a prayer of getting the money."

Matt shook his head and clicked the television back on. "It's your life. Don't come crying to me later."

"You'll be the one crying to me in a few years. Once you've had your fill of unlimited freedom, you'll be back, begging to be a partner."

Matt hooted. "In your dreams."

"Care to make a little wager? A hundred bucks says you'll be back within ten years," Gib said.

"Oh, man, the easiest hundred I'll ever make."

Gib glanced at his grandfather. "Want to set the odds?"

Pete laughed. "No, I think I'll stay out of this one. Now, turn that game back on—your brother's about to lose ten dollars to me."

"WE'VE GOT SO MUCH FOOTAGE we could make an hour-long documentary if we wanted." Izzy sat across the table from Shelly, enjoying brunch at a supper club down the road. Their plates were piled with prime rib, baked potatoes, scrambled eggs, pancakes, fresh melon and pineapple. "The only thing left to shoot is the tunnel—"

"Yeah, and you notice none of the Murphys have mentioned showing it to us since the day it first came up."

"We haven't brought it up to them, either," Izzy pointed out.

Shelly picked up her goblet of orange juice. "I don't know about you, but the last thing I want is for people who may be involved in organized crime to think I'm nosing around in their business. Don't need any bad karma interrupting the flow of good energy toward me getting a new career in film."

"It's so hard to believe. They're such nice, down-to-earth people."

"Especially Beautiful Boy." Shelly rested her elbows on the table and swirled the juice in her glass, taking a sip without saying a word.

Izzy squirmed under her scrutiny. "Now what?" she asked defensively.

"Just wondering where Gib Murphy fits in."

"Into what?"

"Your life."

Izzy felt a dull ache behind her breastbone. "There's no room for him—" She broke off as the waitress refilled their coffee cups and delivered butter pats, sour cream and warm syrup to the table.

"Anything else I can get you?" the woman asked.

"Some antistatins," Izzy muttered.

"I'll have another orange juice," Shelly said. She motioned at Izzy. "Bring her one, too, she needs it." She poured a liberal amount of syrup on her stack of pancakes, then took a bite and chewed thoughtfully. "Gib?" she asked, bringing the conversation back to center.

"I'm following my dreams." Izzy put four pats of butter and all her sour cream on her potato and shoved a big forkful of it in her mouth. If this was the direction their conversation was going to take today, she deserved every ounce of high-fat food she could find, even if she lost their weight-loss contest in the end. "You going to use your sour cream?" she asked.

"Help yourself." Shelly slid the container toward her.

"I'm going to make movies," Izzy said defensively.

"I'm with you, sister. Just wanted to check." Shelly raised her nearly empty glass of orange juice. "Here's to movie premieres and red carpets and dreams."

Dreams. For about the tenth time since yesterday, Izzy relived the conversation she'd had with Gib, about how he wanted to stay and run the resort. And for about the tenth time since yesterday, guilt stabbed at her. "I think I talked Gib out of his dream of running the resort."

"I thought you told him you liked the idea."

"Vaguely. But I also raised objections." She put an elbow on the table and dropped her head into her hand. "It's so convoluted. I didn't want to see him get hurt if the bank refused the loan—which they probably will. I didn't think he should stay just because he couldn't bring himself to take pictures again. And…" She hesitated, not wanting to admit the next part and knowing she had to. "I didn't want him to want to stay."

"Because then your family would be responsible for destroying his dreams."

Tears pricked at the back of Izzy's eyes. "He asked me for an unbiased opinion. I still owe him one." Her thoughts began to gel into a plan of action. "And I owe him the truth. He needs to know that I think his plan for revitalizing the resort is great. And, he needs to know who I really am."

GIB HAD MOWED ABOUT HALF of the resort lawn when he spotted his grandmother waving at him from the lodge veranda. He killed the engine and pulled the MP3 player earbud from his right ear.

"Honey, can you come here a minute?" she called as she hurried toward him.

A well-dressed man followed close on her heels. Gib eyed his khaki shorts, faded polo shirt and sockless running shoes. His clothes were too purposely worn, his sandy-blond hair too studied casual. Obviously the guy was plenty self-impressed. Gib untied his T-shirt from the handle of the mower and used it to wipe the sweat off his face, then pulled it on.

His grandmother reached him before he'd even taken four steps in her direction. "What's up?" he asked.

"This gentleman is looking for someone he thought was staying here," she said, barely above a whisper. "Elizabeth Gordon."

Gib jerked back involuntarily and settled his gaze on the man. "She had a reservation, but canceled the day she was supposed to arrive."

"That's what your grandmother said. But I'm sure she's staying here. I just talked to Izzy a couple of days ago."

Izzy? The world seemed to stop, as if it had been freeze-framed.

"Izzy?" his grandmother asked.

"Her nickname. You sure she's not here? She's making a movie about gangsters."

The guy kept talking, but Gib didn't hear anything else for several seconds. He had to force himself to concentrate so his brain would begin functioning again.

"*Trying* to make a movie, more like it," the man was

saying. "Even though she doesn't have the first notion what she's doing."

Gib had the irrational urge to smash his fist into the guy's face.

"Izzy Stuart," his grandmother choked out. "We have an Izzy Stuart. Making a documentary."

The man's face brightened. "That's my Izzy. Stuart's her middle name. Can you steer me toward her cottage? I'm her fiancé."

IZZY HURRIED TOWARD THE LODGE, her strides lengthening to a light jog. She couldn't wait to find Gib and clear the air about yesterday's discussion. Couldn't wait to get everything in the open, for him to know she was Elizabeth Gordon. She spied him on the front lawn with his grandmother and another man, and slowed her steps so she didn't interrupt their conversation. Gib didn't seem to be paying attention, his head turned like he was listening, but distracted.

Seconds later, Catherine spotted her and said something and both men immediately turned in her direction.

Her heart stopped and her thoughts began to race. No. It couldn't be Andrew. He couldn't possibly have come here. She'd told him not to. He said he wouldn't. Didn't he have to work? What day was it? The days were all running together here. Oh, God, it was *Sunday*. He didn't anchor on Sunday.

"Izzy," he called. He took several steps toward her, mouth curved in that dazzlingly perfect white smile.

Every muscle froze, her breath lodged in her throat. This wasn't how today was supposed to happen. She threw a panicked look at Gib and could see the accusation in his expression, the anger in the set of his jaw. As she started toward them, Andrew misunderstood and opened his arms wide.

She sidestepped him and focused on Gib. "I can explain."

He held up a palm, the muscles in his arm tense beneath the shimmer of perspiration. Yesterday that hand had welcomed her to him—today it held her back.

"No need. Your *fiancé* pretty much explained everything. I get it," he said.

"No, you don't." She controlled the urge to slap Andrew's tanning-booth-bronzed face. "He's not my fiancé."

"Elizabeth Gordon." Gib stepped so close she could smell the gasoline on his hands and the sweat on his skin, and for a second she had the absurd thought that he was going to take her in his arms and kiss away this massive misunderstanding.

And then he strode past her across the lawn, up the steps to the veranda and into the lodge. Her throat was so tight she couldn't speak. She stood there, rooted to the ground, feeling her face grow hot and her heart heavy. All she wanted to do was to get away from here. Tears pricked at her eyes and she turned to his grandmother. The woman hadn't moved a muscle in minutes. "I'm so sorry."

"Best to let it go. The damage is done." Catherine followed Gib to the house.

"Izzy," Andrew said.

She glared at him, the man whose appearance had been no less destructive than a grenade launched into a crowd. At least he'd had the intelligence to keep his mouth shut through the rest of the exchange. "Andrew," she said with barely restrained hostility as she struggled to find the right words. "I hate— I hate French manicures. In fact, when you're not around, I bite my nails." She vigorously bobbed her head. "Uh-huh. And that plaid skirt you bought me just like the one your mother has? I didn't lose it—I gave it to Goodwill. I haven't worn lipstick since I got here a week ago and I love it."

"Izzy, get control of yourself."

Too late, she thought. *The cows have left the barn.* "Not only that, but I adore wearing flip-flops and making that flapping noise. In public. Especially with the cheap rubber ones that cost a dollar at the discount store."

He pulled his back ramrod straight and said, "It has become infinitely clear that we don't suit. I think it best if we considered this relationship…finished." He marched toward the silver Lexus parked in front of the lodge, and with one backward glance after Gib, Izzy headed in the direction of her cottage.

THE MUSIC THROUGH HIS HEADSET was so loud, Gib couldn't hear the lawn mower. Once Izzy and her fiancé had disappeared, he came out to finish cutting the grass, purposely jacking up the sound on his MP3 player so it blocked out the rest of the world.

As if, somehow, the din could prevent what had just happened from hurting him.

Izzy Stuart was Elizabeth Gordon. Her family owned the land. She'd been lying to him since the day she got here.

What had the past week been all about? Was the

documentary a front so she could snoop around? Or was she really trying to break into the film business? Why did she cancel her original reservation and lie about who she was?

Who the hell cared?

As he pushed the mower, he felt a hint of fall in the air, a touch of coolness in the breeze, like a caution, a warning not to get caught unprepared by the change.

No, he would never be caught unprepared again. This afternoon had shown him how much he'd let his guard down this past week. His gaze drifted upward and locked on two hawks soaring high above. A tap on his arm jerked him back to reality and he turned around, startled. *Izzy.*

What did she want now? He killed the engine and pulled out his earbuds.

IZZY SWALLOWED HARD. She'd come back determined to make things right with Gib. But now, facing him, seeing the coldness in his eyes, she was filled with fear that nothing she said would make a difference. "I'm so sorry. I wanted to tell you who I am, but…" How could she say she'd been coming here to tell him everything half an hour ago; it would sound like the worst kind of self-serving lie. Even she didn't believe it and she knew it was true.

"Why'd you come to White Bear?" he asked, his voice glacial.

"To make the documentary."

"So that's real?"

"Yes. We're finalists in an amateur film contest. I really am hoping to get a career in film."

"So why Izzy Stuart? Why not use your real name?"

"The day we arrived, we overheard you at the beach talking about my family selling the land. You sounded like you despised us—*despised me*." She drew a shaky breath. "I didn't plan to lie. But, after hearing you, I wondered what would happen once you learned who I was. And then, suddenly, Shelly was booking a cottage in her name and, honestly, it seemed like it made sense, that things would be less stressful if none of you knew who I was."

"Thanks." He reached for the starter on the mower.

"That's it?"

"What do you want me to say?"

Something about how he understood and it was okay and they'd still be…friends. That everyone makes mistakes and this wasn't such a big deal. Disappointment landed in her stomach like a rock. "I don't know."

She thought she saw his expression soften, but the warmth was gone as quickly as it had appeared.

"I don't know, either." He pulled the starter and the engine roared to life, the harsh sound like a wall between them.

She felt tears spring to her eyes. It was time to go home.

GIB SPENT THE REST OF THE DAY doing yard work, avoiding his family and embracing his anger until even he was sick of it. Late that night he wandered into his brother's room. Matt lay on his bed reading the latest *Ski* magazine, his downhill equipment propped in the corner. "Getting pumped about Montana?" Gib asked.

"You bet."

Gib ran a hand over the top of the ski. "I remember feeling like that. Maybe it's my age, getting closer to thirty, that made me think I wanted to stay here. You were probably right—if I stayed, I'd end up regretting it."

Matt looked up. "Grandma told me what happened. I'm no expert, but I'm thinking you might want to put off any life decisions for a couple of days."

"What I want shouldn't be the deciding factor here. Grandma's dreaming of retiring to Arizona. And I selfishly decided I wanted the resort. But every way I look at it, it doesn't work. If, by some miracle, the bank agrees to lend me the money to buy the land, I keep the resort, but Grandma and Grampa don't get any money to retire on."

Matt set the open magazine upside down on the bed. "What about working with that developer? It sounded like a decent option before."

Gib sat on the end of the bed. "If we cut a deal and I keep the resort and the property it's on, and he gets the rest—"

"Still no money for Grandma and Grampa."

"Right. And then White Bear would fail, anyway. Once he surrounds us with condos, we'll lose our rustic appeal. If I'm selling tranquility as part of retreats and corporate team-building programs, I can't be delivering a bustling metropolis in the woods."

Matt's forehead wrinkled.

"The only way to get money for their retirement is to get out entirely. Sell the buildings to Jack Taylor and close the doors on White Bear Lodge."

"Shit on your dreams."

Yeah, well, he was getting pretty used to shit. "Like

I said, it shouldn't be about what I want. Grampa and Grandma have been working a long time. For once they deserve to have their dreams come true."

CHAPTER FIFTEEN

"NOT THAT I WANT TO PRESSURE you or anything, but it's been three days since we got back. We need to get going on the documentary again." Shelly power-walked beside Izzy during their lunch break. "Have you heard anything from Gib?"

"After that fiasco?" Izzy swung her arms in rhythm with her long strides. She didn't expect to hear from Gib Murphy ever again. "Gib and I are heading in about as opposite directions as two people can go. He wants to stay in a sleepy town in northern Wisconsin, while I want to be in a city that never sleeps like L.A. or New York. He'll be having cookouts on the beach and giving sailing lessons, while I'll be meeting with famous producers and actors."

"Good. Because I'm ready to break out of weather-girling."

They stopped at a traffic light and waited for a steady stream of cars to pass through the intersection. The light changed, and they stepped into the crosswalk.

Izzy gestured at a restaurant as they passed by. "You and I will be hobnobbing at fashionable eateries, while Gib will be hanging out around that big stone hearth in the lodge. He'll have a wife—" She felt a little queasy.

"And kids, who'll help him run White Bear Lodge and, of course, are proud of how successful he's made the business. And, I'll have a husband, too—" her stomach churned a bit more "—and children who'll…stop by my latest movie set to…wave at me…and are so proud of my career."

She stared down the street, at the cars taking people back and forth in their lives, from home to work to family and back again. "But Gib will struggle to get by. And I'll make so much money that I'll be able to buy a place in the country, lots of acres on a lake, and my kids will spend their weekends building tree forts in the woods and swimming and riding their bikes with friends."

She smiled at the mental image. "And at the end of the day, they'll throw their arms around my husband and me, so tired that we have to carry them to bed. And then we'll go outside and collapse on the porch swing together and listen to the crickets chirp and realize that…realize that…we're so happy…and so lucky to live—"

"Yes?" Shelly prodded.

"In the country," she whispered.

"Sounds an awful lot like White Bear Lodge."

Izzy stared at her friend. "It *is* White Bear Lodge," she said, dumbfounded. "Oh, my God, I'm chasing a dream I don't even want."

"I kind of wondered about that. Especially since you haven't had even five minutes to work on the documentary since we got back."

"I think I fell in love with White Bear Lodge," Izzy said. She looked up at the sliver of blue sky between the tall buildings of downtown St. Louis and thought of the sky framed by majestic pines at Menkesoq Lake.

"I think you fell in love with more than just the lodge."

"That's a bit of a leap," Izzy said defensively. "I only knew him a week." Remembering Gib and what they'd begun, what they could have had, made her heart hurt.

"Sometimes that's all it takes."

"Yeah, well, unrequited love only turns out wonderful in fairy tales."

Shelly let her head fall back as she threw her arms dramatically out to either side. "If you believe this is unrequited love, I have a bridge to sell you."

A truck passed them by, engine rumbling like an upset stomach as it exhaled stinky exhaust. Izzy wrinkled her nose and waited until it was gone. "I apologized to him. He didn't want anything to do with me. And to be honest, I can hardly blame him."

Shelly took Izzy's arm to make her stop walking. "Let me cut to the chase here."

"Sure," Izzy said hesitantly.

"You miss Gib."

She opened her mouth to disagree.

"You miss Gib," Shelly repeated. "You miss the resort. You miss who you became at the resort. *I miss who you became at the resort.* The family needs a new lease—or a new partner. Your parents own the land… Come on, figure this out yourself."

Izzy squinted at her friend. "You think I should offer to become their partner?"

"Brilliant! I only wish I had thought of it myself!"

Even though the idea was ridiculous, she loved Shelly for coming up with it. "Just one problem—it's the teeniest thing." She held her thumb and index finger an inch apart. "The Murphys would run me off the property before the word *hello* even passed my lips."

Shelly set out again. "I seriously doubt that. Not the way Gib took to you. Not the way you took to him. Besides, they can't run you off the property. *Your parents own the land. You're the landlord, remember?*"

Izzy's spirits began to rise. Maybe this wasn't such a ridiculous plan, after all. "If I'm a partner, I can go up there whenever I want."

"You can even live there, if that's your inclination. Walk with Gib in the morning, make love with him on the beach in the afternoon, kiss him good-night under the stars every night…"

"Romantic delusions," Izzy said with a delicious shiver. She let herself consider what it would be like to call White Bear Lodge home, to have a stake in whether the resort succeeded or failed, to be a business partner with the Murphys, *to be with Gib every day.* "I don't know if it will work. Not with both Gib and me there, this thing hanging between us—"

A horn blared and they both jumped.

"That's only cloud cover," Shelly said. "Once it blows off, you'll have beautiful weather—plenty of sunshine, low humidity and pleasant temperatures. Izzy, a partnership with you would give Gib's family exactly what they need. It would give you what you need, too." She frowned. "Unless, that is, your parents already signed a contract to sell."

"They couldn't have. The Murphys have another nine or ten days to match the offer. Until they officially say no, my folks can't do anything."

They stopped outside the door to the cable station.

"I need to think about this. I don't want to make an impulsive decision that I regret later." Izzy reached into her slacks pocket for her cell phone. "Maybe it's time for a call to dear old dad."

"No rush decisions here."

"I merely want to remind him the entire country is in a real estate downturn. And he and Mom don't need the money. Why rush to sell?" Her mind was already racing ahead, planning her trip back to White Bear Lodge.

GIB JERKED AWAKE AS HE HIT the bedroom floor. Pain shot though his shoulder. Breathing hard, he lay still in the darkness, reliving his latest nightmare, a new version of the one he'd come to know so well. The café, the guys, it was the same…and not. Izzy had been there, and she'd held him back from following his friends into the street.

With an exhausted sigh, he pulled himself back onto the bed. He'd thought that once Izzy was gone from the resort, he'd be able to put her out of his thoughts, as well. Obviously, his subconscious had other ideas. He'd had exactly one decent night's sleep since coming home to White Bear—the night Izzy had stayed with him. Now that she was gone, he could only expect more nights like this. He lay back and tried to rest, dozing fitfully as the rising sun brightened the edges of his bedroom shade.

Finally giving up, he sat up and looked around the room, still filled with the pieces of his life from when he last lived here. A poster of Bob Marley on the wall, old baseball caps on the bedpost, pens and pencils in a holder he'd made in middle school shop class, a framed picture on the desk of his parents with him and Matt when they were boys. And on the chair in the corner, an important part of his current life, the black case holding his camera—a case he hadn't opened since the explosion.

He got off the bed and picked up the picture, touched the image of his parents' smiling faces with his index finger. This had been shot right before they'd left for the airport, for the flight that had gone down. They were all so happy, none of them suspecting tragedy lay ahead. His throat tightened and tears pressed into his eyes as memories of earlier years mingled with the new, painful ones that came later. If only they hadn't taken that trip.

He set the picture back on his desk. His mother used to say, *if wishes were horses, beggars would ride.* He'd practically reached adulthood before he fully understood what it meant.

There was no going back; there never was. It would have to be enough that he knew how much they'd loved him and Matt. Izzy's words slipped into his mind: *They'd done the best they could.* That they had. His gaze landed on the black camera case again. He glanced away and pulled the shade to reveal a morning still foggy and mysterious, even as the sun was rising and burning away the shroud of mist. There would be photos out there, striking photos with lighting like this. Peaceful, calming, powerfully beautiful.

He gazed out the window a moment longer, then reached for the case and opened it quickly, as though afraid he might not do it if he took too long. He cradled the black Nikon D3 digital camera in both hands and thought back to the day he'd plunked down the money to buy it. At the time, it had felt like a small fortune.

He let the camera slide into position in his palm, comfortably fitting like a piece of clothing you try on years later and are pleasantly surprised to discover still fits. He took off the lens cap and peered through the viewfinder, framing his desk, Bob Marley, his duffel bag in the corner. The world used to change for him when he saw it through the camera. Disappointment coursed through him. Now it looked no different.

He started to put the camera away, then stopped. What was he doing? With the resort all but out of reach, shooting pictures was his only means of making a living. Even if the view through the lens was no longer magic, it was all he had.

He wrapped his fingers around the camera that had once meant everything to him and went downstairs and out the side door. Already the day was warm, and high in the branches, the birds chatted and twittered. As Gib cut across the front yard, Rascal roused himself from his sunny spot and fell into step beside him. Gib patted his head. "Don't want to miss anything, huh, boy?" The dog wagged his tail and followed Gib down to the beach. The blue fishing boat was tied up to the pier where he'd left it yesterday, but he didn't feel like going out on the lake today. Didn't want to be out there and remember what it had been like kissing Izzy.

He went to the end of the dock and sat down on the bench overlooking the water. Five minutes later, his brother scooted in next to him. "Hey. Saw you sneak out the door. Trying to get out of doing work?"

"Yeah. I learned it from you."

Matt pointed at the camera. "You shooting pictures?"

"Thinking about it."

Matt didn't say anything for several seconds. "Is it hard?"

Gib nodded.

"Anything I can do?"

"Nope. My demons to conquer. I know why I can't, but even the knowing doesn't seem to help. It's like…me shooting pictures again means I've moved on and those guys died for nothing. Like their lives are forgotten."

A fish jumped nearby and he watched the ripples in the water, the only sign it had been there at all.

"You're allowed to move on, you know."

Gib turned the camera over in his hands. "That's what Izzy said. We were talking about the meaning of life. She says it's just…*you do the best you can.*"

"That's cool."

"Yeah. Except three guys died because I had to do the best I could. Had to get the right picture so I kept everyone out—"

"Don't be stupid. That's not what she means. Did you do the best you could to save them?"

"Yeah. But it didn't help."

"What did she say about that?"

Gib pictured Izzy's shining face when she'd told him her meaning of life, the day they'd made love in the woods. "You do the best you can at the time. Sometimes the best you can do is only fifty percent, or eighty percent…"

"Maybe you should listen to her."

Two young boys came onto the beach, screwing

around, wrestling with each other and laughing. "There's my sailing lesson," Matt said. "Catch ya later."

Gib watched Matt and the kids hoist the sail, the white fabric flapping in the soft breeze. *You do the best you can at the time.* Maybe Matt was right; he should listen to Izzy. He turned the Nikon on, took off the lens cap and raised the camera to his eye, focusing on two tiny sparrows on a tree branch. His finger hovered over the shutter button for a moment, then he pressed down and stored the shot in memory. He'd done the best he could. He aimed the camera at a clump of birch trees on the shore, framed the shot and took another photo. Standing, he shouted to Matt. All three guys beside the sailboat grinned and he pressed the shutter button to save the image forever.

It was coming back. He was beginning to see beauty again through the lens—not just things, but life and lines and angles and soft edges and composition. He focused on the boathouse, rotated the camera sideways, fiddled with the lighting, then pressed the button and locked in the picture.

A familiar thrill rushed through him, and the fingers of his left hand curled into a fist of triumph. With Rascal at his heels, he trotted down the dock and up to the lodge, stopping to shoot a picture of his grandmother taking out the garbage.

"What are you doing?" She smoothed her hair back.

He shot another picture. "The best I can."

"Well, we could use a little of your best in the kitchen right now."

"On my way." He took the steps to the veranda two at a time, pausing at the top to zoom in for a close-up shot of the lake. As he went into the lodge, it dawned on him—only one thing would make this moment better. The woman who made it possible.

Izzy.

How could he forgive himself and not her?

SATURDAY MORNING, IZZY PULLED her car to a stop in front of the main lodge and sat there a moment without getting out. She'd timed her arrival so the breakfast dishes would be finished and there would be hours before dinner had to be started. Even with that, she was suddenly beset by doubts. What if they'd already signed an agreement with the developer? What if Gib was still furious with her? What if he hated her? She twisted the rearview mirror to check her appearance and contemplated driving away.

You didn't come here to turn around and go home, she told herself sternly. She bent the mirror back into position, grabbed the manila folder off the front seat and opened the door. Rascal wandered off the porch to greet her, and she stopped to run a trembling hand down his back. "Hey, boy, good to see you again, too. Where's your boss?"

Heart pounding like a woodpecker on an oak tree, she crossed the gravel drive and took the steps to the porch. The door burst open before she got there and Gib's grandmother stood in the doorway, eyes wide.

Even Catherine didn't know what to say to her.

Izzy swallowed hard. "Hi. Is, ah, Gib around?"

A smile softened the surprise on the older woman's face. "He took a load of wood down to the fire pit. Getting ready for the Saturday night welcome cookout.

Go on down there and find him." She hesitated. "It's nice to see you again, Izzy."

"It's nice to see you, too," she said, encouraged at the friendliness in Catherine's welcome. Neither moved, as if each knew there was something more to say. Izzy clenched her fingers nervously. "I'm sorry for all the—"

"No. No harm." Catherine waved a hand at the dog. "Go find Gib," she told him.

Rascal loped across the yard.

"Thanks," Izzy said, "for everything." She followed the dog to the hill leading to the beach and stopped there to watch Rascal nuzzle up to Gib. A light wind blew off the lake, brushed her bare arms and mussed her hair. Rascal began to playfully dig in the sand, shooting it out in every direction until Gib was yelling at him to stop, the kids on the beach were running for cover, and even the Steinmetzes in their usual spot in the shade were holding up their hands to protect their faces.

It felt so good to be back.

As Gib bent to scratch Rascal's ears, she wondered what he would say about her proposal to become partners. What would he say about *her?*

She took the path down the hill, smiling as Rascal left Gib to amble in her direction. Gib watched him for a few seconds, then reached into the golf cart and brought out a black camera, long lens on the front, and aimed it at the dog. Joy surged through her; he was shooting pictures again. Maybe some of Shelly's good karma was coming her way and everything would be all right after all.

She knew the moment he spotted her; he pulled the

camera away from his eyes and stared. Then his obvious shock gave way to a smile. Her heart warmed. "Hi," she called.

"Hello," he said when she got closer.

An awkward silence hung between them. There were so many things she wanted to say, but she didn't know where to begin. She clutched the manila folder, suddenly feeling extremely presumptuous.

"Izzy, hello," Mrs. Steinmetz called. "Tell Shelly that Melvin and I are bonding with nature every morning like she taught us."

"She'll be thrilled." She gestured at the camera in Gib's hand. "You're taking pictures again."

"Yeah, thought I'd preserve this place on film. Decided that once we're gone, we'll want more than just memories and twenty-year-old photos."

"Once you're gone?" Panic made her heart pound. "Have you already partnered with that developer? Sold him the resort?"

"No, but we have an attorney reviewing the proposed contract. Only a matter of time."

"I don't want you to have to leave here." Her words came out sounding childish and naive.

"That's nice of you to say, but we don't have a lot of choice. Money being tight, and all." He shrugged. "Not that I'm passing judgment. It's your parents' land, they can sell whenever they want." He started up the path and she followed him, afraid that this was his subtle way of getting her back to her car and sending her home.

"You have that movie finished yet?" he asked over his shoulder. "I want to be able to say *I knew her when.*"

"No, but we're working on it. Shelly's still gung ho, but I've lost some enthusiasm."

He stopped to face her, incredulous.

"I had an epiphany of sorts," she explained. "I discovered I was chasing down big-time moviemaking for all the wrong reasons."

"Like what?"

"Well…" All her practiced replies suddenly felt totally lame. They reached the top of the hill, and she bent to pick up a stone and roll it in the palm of her hand. "I was making that movie so I could go back to my high school reunion having accomplished my dreams. But dreams change. And I realized what I wanted then isn't what I want now."

When he didn't reply, Izzy pushed forward, her stomach a jumbled mass of nerves. "That's why I'm here. To let you know my parents have decided not to sell the land."

He flinched, almost as if he'd been hit. "What?"

She looked at those gray eyes of his, at that mouth she'd kissed, and she wished he would take her into his arms and tell her he'd missed her these past few days. "I wanted to make sure you knew before you signed an agreement with that developer and ended up with a business partner you didn't need."

"Why aren't they selling?" He went past her car up to the porch.

"You almost sound disappointed."

He shook his head. "I don't know what to think. The only way my grandparents can afford to retire is by selling the resort. If the land isn't for sale, that developer won't want to buy the buildings. My grandparents will be stuck here." He dropped down onto one of the Adirondack chairs. "For their sake, Izzy, I wish your parents *would* sell."

"They can't." She held up the manila folder and realized she was trembling again. "Because…I own the land now. After staying here for ten days, I came to some realizations about myself and my life. I don't want to see a big development on this property. I don't want to see White Bear Lodge disappear. So I convinced my parents—"

"You own the land?" he asked incredulously.

"Bought it for a dollar. My folks don't need the money. They also think I'm crazy—Northwoods rustic isn't their thing. But I think they've finally realized it's okay if I want something different than they do."

"So, what do you want?" He met her gaze and her courage wavered.

"I know your grandparents and brother want to leave," she said softly. "And I know you want to stay. Or, at least, you said you wanted to stay. So what I want is… The thing is, if I keep the land and you keep the resort, I thought… I mean, if you're interested, there's an option… We could be…partners."

He didn't say a word.

"Maybe," she whispered. "I wouldn't have to live here permanently…. I have an idea for your corporate team-building programs. You're going to need someone to videotape group-dynamic things like role-playing and problem solving and…I could do that. I know my way around a camera and I like doing it."

At his lack of response, mortification cascaded through her. Obviously, he didn't know how to tell her that while he might want to keep the resort, he didn't want any part of her. She swallowed down the lump of embarrassment and disappointment that welled up in her throat.

"It's not that simple," he finally said. "For us, for my grandparents, it would be better if you just sold the land. I'd love to consider your offer, but I don't have a choice—"

"Of course you do!" His grandmother's voice floated through the screen door seconds before she pushed it open. "I couldn't help overhearing and it sounds awfully good, Gib."

"Stooping to eavesdropping now, Gram?"

"I was on my way outside. Gib, she might be on to something. You should consider it." Catherine wiped her hands on the dishcloth she was holding.

"If I do, you'll never get to Arizona. I won't do that to you."

She took the chair next to him. "I have a confession to make. I never really wanted to go to Arizona."

Gib's eyes widened. "You don't want to retire?"

"Well, now, that's a little different. I'd like to cut back on the workload, that's for sure. But I never wanted to leave here. I love this place. It's been home ever since your grandfather and I married. I can't picture living somewhere else."

"Then why'd you bring up Arizona?"

She clasped her hands together in her lap and let out a sigh. "Because it was killing your grandfather that we were going to lose the resort. And I figured, rightly, that if he thought I wanted out, it would take away some of the hurt."

"But you won't have any retirement money."

"I've put a little aside for a rainy day. We've got a bit of money—not a lot. But something. Your grandfather doesn't know a thing about it."

Gib looked between his grandmother and Izzy. "Let me repeat this to be sure I have it right. If I keep the resort, you'd be all right with retiring here?"

"It's all I've ever wanted."

"Well, hell." Gib let out a laugh. "We may have something to discuss, after all. Ladies, let's go find Matt and Grampa."

FIFTEEN MINUTES LATER, with all of them gathered in the living room, Izzy explained her proposal.

"What about your documentary?" Matt asked.

"We're going to finish it in the next couple of weeks. Then we'll send it in and hope for the best. No matter what happens, it won't change what I want—to be here."

Gib couldn't keep the smile off his face. "Does anyone have a problem with me going into partnership with the owner of the land?"

"Be my guest." Matt tossed a throw pillow at his brother. "I think you're both nuts. Be honest—have you really considered what you're taking on here?"

Gib looked at Izzy and nodded.

"Yes," she said.

"Because," Matt continued, "without honesty you have nothing. Honesty, you know, is the first chapter in the book of wisdom."

Gib squinted at his brother, dumbfounded. "What?"

"Thomas Jefferson."

"He's right. Honesty is the best policy," his grandfather added.

Gib made a choking noise. "You know, I'm probably the most honest person here. Matt—"

"I'm honest," his brother said.

"Yeah? You lined up a job in Montana, planned to take off this winter and not even tell anyone in advance." Gib placed his attention squarely on his grandfather. "And you. Grampa, you've been running that penny-ante sports betting thing as long as I can remember."

"Ohmigosh, is that what's going on around here?" Izzy burst out.

Pete let his head fall back against his chair. "I gave that up ten years ago. Gib just refuses to believe it."

"I'll believe it once you explain what those *business meetings* you've been having lately are all about."

"I might as well show you." His grandfather left the room, returning a minute later with a large flat package wrapped in brown paper. "Your grandma and I are coming up on being married forty-eight years. So…" He handed Catherine the package and her eyes teared even before she opened it.

"Peter." She took off the paper deliberately, then held up a painting of the lodge, years ago, a young couple standing arm in arm on the front steps.

"I had this done from an old photo," Pete said.

Catherine reached up to cup his cheek with her hand and give him a kiss. "It was the night we got engaged."

Pete sat in the recliner again. "That man who showed up at the cookout? He did the painting. And Butch took care of the framing for me. Sorry about all that…misleading information. I wanted it to be a surprise."

"You succeeded," Gib said. "I guess I owe you an apology." He gestured across the room. "Who would have guessed one family could have all this duplicity? We really need to stop it." He looked at his grandmother. "That means you, too, with that secret savings account—"

"What secret savings account?" Pete sat up straight and turned to his wife.

She opened her eyes wide, as though surprised by the question. "It's our retirement fund."

"How'd you do that?"

"I, ah, paid myself first—like the experts tell you to do. We won't be able to retire in style, but it's something. I never told you about it because I knew you'd want to spend it on the resort. And we needed to be prepared for a rainy day or old age, whichever came first."

Gib placed his gaze squarely on Izzy. "As for you—"

"Believe me, I have plenty of regrets," she said. "I am so sorry about everything. But hopefully the solution will make up for the deception. Now that everything's on the table, can we forget all that?"

He held her gaze for a long moment, watched her beautiful face watching him expectantly. There was not one ounce of residual anger left in him. Only love.

Love.

He had fallen in love with Izzy Gordon.

"Everything's not on the table yet. Come on, Iz, we need to talk in private." He started for the door without waiting for her, went down the stairs and outside onto the veranda. There could be no talk of a business partnership until they came to a conclusion about what had taken place between them. His stomach jumped nervously. He didn't just want Izzy working at the front desk or in the kitchen, he wanted her in his bed and at his side, a full partner. This was the woman he wanted to spend the rest of his life with.

He stopped in front of the porch swing. "There's something we have to clarify before we make any decision about a partnership."

"I know I should have told you from the beginning who I was."

He shook his head. "Not important. I mean it's important, but I understand why you did it. The thing is, Izzy, I think a partnership would be great, but—" He struggled to find the right words. "Owning a resort is demanding. Especially during the peak season. I don't want to take on a partner who decides in six months that this place ties her down too much."

She looked away from him, out over the property. "When Shelly and I left here, I thought everything would be fine once I went to work again. But back in my beige cubicle, in an office filled with beige cubicles, no windows except at the outer reaches, fluorescent lighting overhead, and the clock ticking off every hour of the workday, I couldn't stay focused."

She raised her eyes to his, and he had to shove his hands in his pockets to keep from pulling her into his arms.

"I kept remembering White Bear Lodge. The lake, the grounds, even that run-down cottage we stayed in. That's when I realized I felt alive here, that this was what I wanted." Her lips curved up a tiny bit. "I knew I could never live with myself if I was responsible for this land being developed. But..."

"What?"

"But how about you, Gib? You're not staying here to run away from your pain, are you? Because I don't want a partner who decides in six months that this was a nice place to rest and lick his wounds, but now the rest of the world beckons and adios, senorita."

He felt like he was taking part in an exquisite dance, each of them following the same steps, just not quite in rhythm with each other yet. "I've given this a lot of thought," he said cautiously. "I picked up my camera for the first time two days ago, have been shooting pictures every day. It feels comfortable, like I've closed a door that was swinging loose. But it's not what I want to do anymore—at least not full-time." *Not if I'm with you.*

He knew he had to go for it or explode. "Oh, hell, Izzy, it's you. It's all because of you. You gave me the first good night's sleep I'd had in months. You're the reason I was able to put that camera to my eye and push the shutter button. You made me see what life is about—"

"You do the best you can," she said. "It's harder to learn than it is to say."

A long, weighted silence stretched between them.

"You make me want to do the best I can every day," he said. "I love you, Izzy Gordon. I started loving you the night you called the cops when I was digging night crawlers. But I didn't realize it until you were gone."

Inside the lodge, the telephone began to ring.

Izzy clasped her hands together in front of her chest. "I love you, too," she whispered. "I was afraid I'd ruined it. That it was too late—"

"No. Never too late."

The phone kept ringing and Gib glanced at the screen door. From inside, his grandmother called out, "I'll get it." He heard the click of her shoes on the hardwood floor as she hurried toward the phone at the front desk.

"So…" Izzy's eyes took on a sparkle. "Do you agree? Should we go into partnership, then?"

"Only if we're partners in every sense of the word." He kissed her then with all the love in his heart, this woman who had given him back his life. "For the rest of our lives."

"White Bear Lodge. Can I help you?" he heard his grandmother say. "Yes, let me get my ledger."

Izzy raised her brows.

"That's ten on the Yankees, ten on the Dodgers and twenty on the Brewers," his grandmother said. "Okay, you're all set. Good luck."

"At least now you know your grandfather was telling the truth," Izzy said.

"I need to put a stop to this right now."

Izzy's arms tightened around him. "There's plenty of time for that later. Right now, I want to hear more about this complete partnership you're proposing."

He thought to himself there wasn't anyone he'd rather be with, that no matter what life decided to throw at them, with Izzy at his side they'd beat the odds. He bent to kiss her again. "Izzy Stuart Gordon, without a doubt you're the best bet I'll ever take."

* * * * *

*Celebrate 60 years of pure reading pleasure
with Harlequin®!*

To commemorate the event, Silhouette Special
Edition invites you to Ashley O'Ballivan's bed-
and-breakfast in the small town of Stone Creek.
The beautiful innkeeper will have her hands full
caring for her old flame Jack McCall. He's on the
run and recovering from a mysterious illness, but
that won't stop him from trying to win Ashley back.

*Enjoy an exclusive glimpse of Linda Lael Miller's
AT HOME IN STONE CREEK
Available in November 2009 from
Silhouette Special Edition®*

The helicopter swung abruptly sideways in a dizzying arch, setting Jack McCall's fever-ravaged brain spinning.

His friend's voice sounded tinny, coming through the earphones. "You belong in a hospital," he said. "Not some backwater bed-and-breakfast."

All Jack really knew about the virus raging through his system was that it wasn't contagious, and there was no known treatment for it besides a lot of rest and quiet. "I don't like hospitals," he responded, hoping he sounded like his normal self. "They're full of sick people."

Vince Griffin chuckled but it was a dry sound, rough at the edges. "What's in Stone Creek, Arizona?" he asked. "Besides a whole lot of nothin'?"

Ashley O'Ballivan was in Stone Creek, and she was a whole lot of somethin', but Jack had neither the strength nor the inclination to explain. After the way he'd ducked out six months before, he didn't expect a welcome, knew he didn't deserve one. But Ashley, being Ashley, would take him in whatever her misgivings.

He had to get to Ashley; he'd be all right.

He closed his eyes, letting the fever swallow him.

There was no telling how much time had passed when he became aware of the chopper blades slowing overhead. Dimly, he saw the private ambulance waiting on the airfield outside of Stone Creek; it seemed that twilight had descended.

Jack sighed with relief. His clothes felt clammy against his flesh. His teeth began to chatter as two figures unloaded a gurney from the back of the ambulance and waited for the blades to stop.

"Great," Vince remarked, unsnapping his seat belt. "Those two look like volunteers, not real EMTs."

The chopper bounced sickeningly on its runners, and Vince, with a shake of his head, pushed open his door and jumped to the ground, head down.

Jack waited, wondering if he'd be able to stand on his own. After fumbling unsuccessfully with the buckle on his seat belt, he decided not.

When it was safe the EMTs approached, following Vince, who opened Jack's door.

His old friend Tanner Quinn stepped around Vince, his grin not quite reaching his eyes.

"You look like hell warmed over," he told Jack cheerfully.

"Since when are you an EMT?" Jack retorted.

Tanner reached in, wedged a shoulder under Jack's right arm and hauled him out of the chopper. His knees immediately buckled, and Vince stepped up, supporting him on the other side.

"In a place like Stone Creek," Tanner replied, "everybody helps out."

They reached the wheeled gurney, and Jack found himself on his back.

Tanner and the second man strapped him down, a process that brought back a few bad memories.

"Is there even a hospital in this place?" Vince asked irritably from somewhere in the night.

"There's a pretty good clinic over in Indian Rock," Tanner answered easily, "and it isn't far to Flagstaff." He paused to help his buddy hoist Jack and the gurney into the back of the ambulance. "You're in good hands, Jack. My wife is the best veterinarian in the state."

Jack laughed raggedly at that.

Vince muttered a curse.

Tanner climbed into the back beside him, perched on some kind of fold-down seat. The other man shut the doors.

"You in any pain?" Tanner said as his partner climbed into the driver's seat and started the engine.

"No." Jack looked up at his oldest and closest friend and wished he'd listened to Vince. Ever since he'd come down with the virus—a week after snatching a five-year-old girl back from her non-custodial parent, a small-time Colombian drug dealer—he hadn't been able to think about anyone or anything but Ashley. When he *could* think, anyway.

Now, in one of the first clearheaded moments he'd experienced since checking himself out of Bethesda the day before, he realized he might be making a major mistake. Not by facing Ashley—he owed her that much and a lot more. No, he could be putting her in danger, putting Tanner and his daughter and his pregnant wife in danger, too.

"I shouldn't have come here," he said, keeping his voice low.

Tanner shook his head, his jaw clamped down hard as though he was irritated by Jack's statement.

"This is where you belong," Tanner insisted. "If you'd had sense enough to know that six months ago, old buddy, when you bailed on Ashley without so much as a fare-thee-well, you wouldn't be in this mess."

Ashley. The name had run through his mind a million times in those six months, but hearing somebody say it out loud was like having a fist close around his insides and squeeze hard.

Jack couldn't speak.

Tanner didn't press for further conversation.

The ambulance bumped over country roads, finally hitting smooth blacktop.

"Here we are," Tanner said. "Ashley's place."

* * * * *

Will Jack be able to patch things up with Ashley,
or will his past put the woman he loves
in harm's way?
Find out in
AT HOME IN STONE CREEK
by Linda Lael Miller
Available November 2009 from
Silhouette Special Edition®.

This November,
Silhouette Special Edition®
brings you

NEW YORK TIMES
BESTSELLING AUTHOR

LINDA LAEL MILLER

At Home in
Stone Creek

Available in November
wherever books are sold.

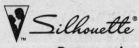

This November,
queen of the rugged rancher

PATRICIA THAYER

teams up with

DONNA ALWARD

to bring you an extra-special treat
this holiday season—

two romantic stories
in one book!

Join sisters Amelia and Kelley for Christmas at
Rocking H Ranch where these feisty cowgirls swap
presents for proposals, mistletoe for marriage and
experience the unbeatable rush of falling in love!

Available in November wherever books are sold.

REQUEST YOUR FREE BOOKS!

2 FREE NOVELS PLUS 2 FREE GIFTS!

HARLEQUIN®

Super Romance®

Exciting, emotional, unexpected!

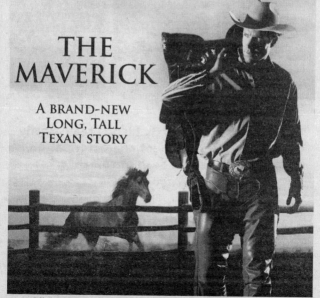

Silhouette Desire

**FROM *NEW YORK TIMES*
BESTSELLING AUTHOR**

DIANA
PALMER

THE
MAVERICK

**A BRAND-NEW
LONG, TALL
TEXAN STORY**

 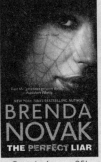 

COMING NEXT MONTH

Available November 10, 2009

#1596 LIKE FATHER, LIKE SON • Karina Bliss
The Diamond Legacy

What's worse? Discovering his heritage is a lie or following in his grandfather's footsteps? All Joe Fraser *does* know is that Philippa Browne is pregnant and he's got to do right by her. Too bad she has her own ideas about motherhood…and marriage

#1597 HER SECRET RIVAL • Abby Gaines
Those Merritt Girls

Taking over her father's law firm isn't just the professional opportunity of a lifetime—it's a chance for Megan Merritt to finally get close to him. Winning a lucrative divorce case is her way to prove she's the one for the job. Except the opposing lawyer in the divorce is Travis Jamieson, who is also after her dad's job!

#1598 A CONFLICT OF INTEREST • Anna Adams
Welcome to Honesty

Jake Sloane knows right from wrong—as a judge, it's his responsibility. Until he meet Maria Keaton, he's never blurred that line. Now his attraction to her is tearing him between what his head knows he should do and what his heart wants.

#1599 HOME FOR THE HOLIDAYS • Sarah Mayberry
Single Father

Raising his kids on his own is a huge learning curve for Joe Lawson. So does he really have time to fall for the unconventional woman next door, Hannah Napier? Time or no that's what's happening.…

#1600 A MAN WORTH LOVING • Kimberly Van Meter
Home in Emmett's Mill

Aubrey Rose can't stand Sammy Halvorsen when they first meet. She agrees to be a nanny to his infant son only because she's a sucker for babies. As she gets to know Sammy, however, she starts to fall for him. But how to make him realize he's a man worth loving?

#1601 UNEXPECTED GIFTS • Holly Jacobs
9 Months Later

Elinore Cartright has her hands full overseeing the teen parenting program, especially when she discovers *she's* unexpectedly expecting. Not how she envisioned her forties, but life's unpredictable. So is her friend Zac Keller, who suddenly wants to dat her *and* be a daddy, too!

HSRCNMBPA1009